"You should sleep."

His orders were getting a bit out of hand, but she let it pass. He'd killed for her. When a guy took that step, you cut him some slack.

"I'm not getting into bed before I wash the dirt and blood and heaven only knows what else off me."

His gaze wandered all over her, and the skin under his heated gaze tingled. "What about you? You can have half of the bed."

"No. It's not a good idea."

"I was only talking about getting some rest. Nothing else."

"You know, you're a very attractive woman, Sela."

"One with her own mind. I know who I'm attracted to and who I'm not."

"And what type of guy are you attracted to?"

She debated playing it safe, then thought about how close she'd come to death over the last twenty-four hours, and skipped right over the games to the truth.

"You."

HELENKAY DIMON

THE BIG GUNS

TORONTO NEW YORK LONDON
AMSTERDAM PARIS SYDNEY HAMBURG
STOCKHOLM ATHENS TOKYO MILAN MADRID
PRAGUE WARSAW BUDAPEST AUCKLAND

To Jill Shalvis for being a terrific conference roommate, enthusiastic first reader and great friend.

Recycling programs
for this product may
not exist in your area.

ISBN-13: 978-0-373-69570-6

THE BIG GUNS

Copyright © 2011 by HelenKay Dimon

www.Harlequin.com

Printed in U.S.A.

Chapter One

Sela Andrews was five minutes away from walking into an ambush. Slumped down in his Jeep on the street outside her apartment, Zach Bachman watched the setup unfold.

The small split-screen monitor on his watch showed Sela approaching the elevator on the floor five stories above.

That wasn't the problem, except for how clueless she appeared to be to the danger around her. The other shot centered on the building's underground garage. There, in stall seventeen, not far from where Zach sat, a man fiddled with something under the hood of her car.

And not just any man. A guy dressed in black, his gaze skipping around the garage as if looking for witnesses. He'd even taken the time to disable the security camera. He just didn't know he'd missed one—Zach's.

Thanks to this development, Zach knew he had to break his word. When he'd convinced Adam Wright, his fellow Recovery Project agent, to tap into the cameras in Sela's building, Zach promised to watch but not get involved. That wasn't possible now. He pressed the

green button on the bottom of his watch and sent Adam
an emergency pulse. Just in case.

That left Sela. Going through the garage door was
the faster route to cutting her off, but also the most
likely to give away his position and get shot. Not his
favorite activity, certainly not at this painfully early
time of day. No, he had to do this the long and hard way.

Out of the car, he hit the building's lobby at a run,
stopping only to use the master key Adam had made
for just this type of problem. Zach's sneakers squeaked
against the tile floor as he crossed in front of the elevator bank. He knew the schematics without thinking and
headed for the emergency stairwell in the back corner.

As he raced down the stairs two at a time to the
underground garage, his palm slid against the metal
railing. The stale hot air of the enclosed space filled his
lungs, but he didn't stop. As they passed, he ignored the
man stumbling up the stairs from what looked like a
hard night of drinking. None of that mattered because
Zach had to get there before she did.

He hit the landing, stopping only when momentum
slammed his shoulder against the stairwell door. His
breathing stayed steady and strong, a testament to his
former military career and good conditioning.

He pressed his hand against the door and waited for
the ding of the elevator bell to signal Sela's entry into
the garage.

Only silence greeted him.

The door creaked as he pulled it open and peered
into the dark garage through the tiny slit. Nothing. Too
much nothing. Everything was quiet.

No squealing tires. No engines running. At just after four in the morning on a summer weekend, no one else was in the garage. Not even a security guard. That might be usual for some parts of the country, but not for a city. This area of D.C. buzzed with some level of activity most of the time, but not this morning.

The emergency cones set up at the garage's entrance likely played a role in that. Looked like this guy had thought of everything to give him the precious time needed to get to Sela. The real concern centered on the guy knowing Sela would be on the move in the early-morning hours on a Sunday. Zach had watched her for weeks and hadn't anticipated her going out now. But this guy knew.

Not wanting to be too many steps behind, Zach slipped into the garage, keeping his back flat against the concrete wall. With one hand he caught the door before it slammed shut behind him. With the other he reached for the gun tucked into the holder on his hip.

Then he saw it. Behind a row of cars, something flashed. Possibly nothing, but just as likely a reflection of the attacker from all the metal overhead. It gave Zach a place to focus.

He slid down against the wall, debating whether to make his move and take the attacker out before he touched Sela or hold his position. The elevator bell ruined any chance of an offensive strike. He had no choice. The most dangerous option won out.

With a harsh hiss of profanity, he slunk back into the shadows. His insides screamed to grab Sela to safety, but his head knew the right answer. Bide his time.

This—whatever was happening right now—could be the key to finding the information he needed on Trevor Walters, Sela's boss, and the Recovery Project's nemesis.

Zach couldn't stop now, not when he was this close to his goal. He'd made a personal vow to find the evidence needed to catch Trevor once and for all, and Zach meant to keep it.

Sela stepped into the garage. Folders and paperwork weighed down her arms. Her sandy-blond hair fell loose in gentle curls around her shoulders. She hummed an off-key tune, seemingly oblivious to the choking gas fumes in the enclosed space.

Zach shook his head at her behavior. For a smart woman she acted pretty dumb. With her arms full, she couldn't defend herself. Now he had to handle the job.

Moving in double time, she put a slim file between her teeth and wrestled her car keys out of the pocket of her black blazer. While juggling books and papers in one arm, she aimed the door opener at her car. The high-pitched chirp of the alarm echoed through the abandoned garage.

Zach shifted, trying to figure out the current location of the owner of the mysterious glint of light. When he glanced back at Sela, he realized the worst had happened. Her attacker had managed to sneak up on her, his cover protected thanks to her awful pseudosinging and the bulky back end of her SUV.

When she reached for the door handle, balancing her load on an upraised thigh, her stalker sprang into action. A metal object swooped down in an arc before connecting with her head. Zach jumped at the resounding whack as he watched her crumple to the cement. Papers fell in a swoosh and scattered. Her keys jangled, then skidded to a halt under her SUV. She didn't have warning or time to scream.

The only sound came from the attacker a second later. "Got her," he said into his cell phone, not bothering to lower his voice.

Zach muttered a harsh oath under his breath but forced his legs to remain still. His hands clenched and unclenched as he watched the attacker stuff Sela's unmoving body into a rusty pickup truck parked a few spots away from hers. Slipping the small camera out of his pocket, he took the attacker's photo. Got a shot of the truck, too. When the vehicle roared to life and started moving, Zach flipped into fast-forward. He hesitated only until the guy pulled away and out of sight, then Zach ran out of the garage entrance and up the ramp into the warm, dark morning.

In a silent crouch, he headed for the Jeep. It took less than a minute to get there and slide inside. The ignition turned over with little more than a soft purr. Leaving the lights off, he followed the truck at a safe distance, hanging back behind the few other cars on the road.

Keeping his gaze on the license plate in front of him, Zach hit the button on his watch to patch him into Recovery Project headquarters. Adam picked up on the first ring. He was the tech guy in their group. He had a series of cameras set up throughout the city and could track anything or anyone who was moving.

Before Adam could say a word, Zach jumped in. "I'm sending you a photo."

"That's nice of you. Thanks for dragging me out of bed, by the way."

"I need an ID."

"Got it." The amusement left Adam's voice this time. "This looks bad."

"Also need you to do your satellite magic and follow a car for me in case I lose it. Track me and then look for the truck a short distance in front of me."

"It's not as easy as you make it sound, but I'll figure it out."

"And I can't explain now, so don't ask." Zach hung up without any other discussion, knowing Adam would make it all work.

The rest, like saving the girl, was up to Zach.

SELA'S HEAD THROBBED. The muscles in her upper arms burned in agony. Her right cheek felt raw and puffy. Every part of her body, except maybe her nose, hurt like never before.

She tried to sit up but flopped back down when the world spun violently around her. Her hands weren't bound, but the blinding soreness coursing through her body made even small movements difficult.

She remembered bits and pieces of the last few minutes. She'd gathered up her work and ran out of her apartment without doing her usual check. The rush to talk to her boss made her less than careful. Normally, that wouldn't be a problem. She lived in Foggy Bottom, a nice part of Washington, D.C., home to a university, the infamous Watergate and Kennedy Center and rows of impressive brownstones.

But she had known someone was watching her. Could feel the eyes focus on her every time she stepped out her door, which was why she was headed to the office before dawn, before the city burst to life. Her nerves had buzzed until all she heard was a chaotic melody in her head. She remembered the garage and a crack against her skull. She bounced around a vehicle until her kidnapper treated her to another fist to the side of the head.

She'd experienced more violence in the past hour—or maybe minutes, she wasn't even sure how much time has passed—than in her entire life up until that point. The good news, what little she could find, came from her ability to breathe. Whoever hit her hadn't killed her. The only question was how long her good fortune would hold out.

"Mornin', sunshine." The feral voice shocked her into opening her sore eyes.

The brightness sent a new bolt of pain ricocheting around the inside of her brain. The harsh glow from the overhead light screamed through the room and forced her out of her slumber. She saw her attacker face-to-face and immediately missed the false safety of darkness.

A squeal raced to her lips, but she swallowed it back down. Greasy brown hair, narrow yellow-brown eyes and a dirt-stained blue jean jacket. The burly vermin balanced in front of her on his haunches, his stale breath hissing against the bruised skin on her face.

He was her nightmare.

Heck, he was every woman's nightmare.

"Wake up, sweetie pie. It's time for us to have some fun."

She ignored his grim words as her gaze darted around the room. She needed an escape or something big enough to knock him over.

"What's the matter? You not gonna talk?" His booming laugh filled the small space as he leaned in closer.

What he found so funny, she had no idea.

"I could make you talk. Scream for me, even." Instead of following through with his threat, he pushed against his thighs and stood.

Sela let out the shaky breath suspended in her chest. From what she could see, she was in a one-room cabin with two possible exits—a window above the kitchen sink that was caked with filth, and the front door off to her left. A very solid-looking wooden door and she had to go through a disgusting guy to get there.

A metal card table and two folding chairs sat in front of the kitchenette lining the wall to her far right. The path to the front door looked miles away, even though the room could not have been more than fifteen feet wide.

She tried a second time to heave her aching body to a sitting position when a brisk knock at the front door stopped her. Her captor whipped out a small gun from behind his back and aimed it in the direction of the sound. Before Sela could scream for help he grabbed her shoulder and lifted her off the sofa.

The jarring move sent a new wave of pain rattling through her battered body. She whimpered but her captor silenced any sound by locking his elbow around her neck and dragging her, half-choking, across the room.

With his back against the door and the muzzle of his gun pressed against her forehead, he called out. "Who is it?"

"Open up," came the muffled reply.

Sela struggled to identify the voice. From her attacker's frown, she assumed he couldn't place it, either.

Her attacker's grip eased enough for circulation to rush back to her neck. She debated whether or not she could land a swift kick in this guy's crotch. The idea of him falling to the ground in agony sure sounded good right about now.

"Johnnie? Let me in." The door muffled the other man's voice but his words were clear.

Her captor pressed the tip of the gun against the wooden door. "Who are you?"

"The boss sent me."

"Not possible."

Boss? The contents of Sela's stomach spun and swished. The situation went from awful to unbelievable. She had to get out of there, and having two attackers wasn't going to make that easy.

"This is your final warning. Open up," the mystery guest yelled through the door.

When Johnnie unlocked the door, Sela felt the last of her hope shrivel.

Chapter Two

Zach heard the lock click and nearly ripped the cabin door off its hinges in the rush to get to Sela. He surged through the door and stopped. His gun never wavered. It aimed right at Johnnie's forehead in a weapons standoff.

Adam had tracked this guy, Johnnie Weed, down and sent over his criminal record via secured text. Sounded like Johnnie liked to hurt women. Zach decided on the race through back roads that he wouldn't need backup to take care of Johnnie if he touched Sela. He would tear the other man apart with his bare hands.

Right now the shock on Johnnie's face matched the fear on Sela's. "I don't know you," Johnnie said.

Zach forced his lungs to inflate, then slowly released his held breath. His gaze moved over her, checking for any sign of injury. A fierce bruise already marred her cheek. Her short skirt was hiked up high on her thighs, and it looked as if her scuffed pumps were the only things holding her tattered panty hose to her legs.

Rage filled his brain until he had to fight the urge to kill Johnnie right there. Instead, Zach nodded in Sela's direction with a studied coolness he didn't feel. "Let her go."

Johnnie kept his arm locked around her slim throat as he held her just out of Zach's easy reach. "This ain't your business."

Johnnie's gun shifted next to her face. Zach concentrated on the weapon so he didn't have to see the confusion move over her.

Yeah, she knew him. He could tell by the way her eyes narrowed and her mouth fell into a grim line. Identifying him sure didn't mean she was happy to see him. She looked the exact opposite of relieved.

And Zach could guess why. The Recovery Project made it a priority to discover everything about Trevor Walters and it would be dumb to assume he didn't return the favor. Zach guessed his team's photos were all over Trevor's office and since Sela was Trevor's assistant she knew all the details.

"Put that thing down before you hurt her." Zach issued the order as he plotted a way to inflict some hurt of his own on Johnnie.

"Why do you get a say?"

"Just do it."

"Do ya think you're in charge?"

Zach's hand snaked out with lightning speed. He grabbed the barrel of Johnnie's gun and snatched it away. With the other arm, Zach elbowed Johnnie under the jaw. The man's head whipped back from the offensive strike, and he lost his grip on Sela. She spun to the side and landed on the dusty floor with a soft groan.

Zach moved in. He slammed Johnnie in the nose

with the heel of his hand. The sudden whack worked as planned. Johnnie howled in pain as blood spurted.

"I'm in charge around here, Johnnie. Don't forget it."

"Why did ya hit me?" The guy practically squealed the question.

"You're lucky that's all I did."

"Did the boss really send you?"

Zach treated Johnnie to a look of disgust. "Clean yourself up."

Johnnie crawled to his feet and grabbed for the dirty kitchen towel hanging over the faucet. "You broke my nose."

Hurting Johnnie felt good. Too good. Zach cursed his lack of control. He'd finally wrestled the animal part of him into submission only to find his hold weak.

Sela picked that moment to make a mad dash for the door. The woman had a lousy sense of timing.

She ducked low and tried to barrel past him. She might have made it, too, except he was ready. He knew she was a born fighter. He'd studied her, followed her and watched her day after day for weeks. The person who ordered her kidnapping might underestimate her survival instinct. Zach didn't plan to make that mistake.

He snatched her around her slim waist and lifted her into the air, pressing her back against the full length of his body with as gentle a touch as possible. "Whoa, you're not going anywhere."

"Let me go." Labored breathing strained her voice.

When he squeezed her midsection, she let out a

shocked yelp of distress. He turned her around so their noses almost touched. "What is it? What's wrong?"

She pushed against him, her small fists knocking against his chest in a futile attempt to break free. "Don't touch me."

Zach captured her hands in his and pulled her body tight against him. Each slope and contour of her fit him like a perfect puzzle piece.

"Settle down," he said.

She ignored him. She grunted and shoved at him.

"Are you hurt?" He conducted a visual tour, looking for signs of obvious injury.

"What do you care?" Her eyes promised mutiny.

"I'll take that as a yes." Zach scowled at Johnnie where he leaned over the nearby sink, and once again debated killing him. "I'll deal with you later."

Zach could not get off his game. Not yet. There would be time to talk and figure out why Johnnie picked today and who hired him, but this wasn't it. Reacting to her distress would distract him and kill them both.

"You touch her, Johnnie, you die. You understand me?"

"Well, well, well." Johnnie threw the stained towel in the sink. "Big man thinks he owns the woman."

Adrenaline pumped through Zach. His only thought was to protect Sela. That was his job. Didn't matter if it was a formal operation or a self-imposed assignment. He'd taken on that role the second he started watching her.

The blow came out of nowhere.

One minute Johnnie skulked around, head down and

shoulders slumped with a general air of defeat. The next he snarled like a wild animal. He aimed his full body weight for Zach's stomach. Anticipating the hit, Zach moved to the side at the last minute and pushed Sela out of the fray.

Johnnie didn't stop. He launched a second strike. This one with fists. Zach blocked a wild punch and sent Johnnie spinning into the couch. Zach outweighed his attacker by a good thirty pounds and he had been trained to fight. Trained by the best to kill.

A kick straight to the stomach and the fight ended with Johnnie rolling on the floor, holding his bruised ribs. In those precious final minutes of battle Zach feared he had gone over the edge, that his tenuous hold on his control had finally snapped, speeding him across that imaginary line between good and evil.

Thinking about Johnnie hurting Sela torched Zach's insides. He barely knew her, but that didn't matter. There were some things a man didn't do. Smacking a woman around was at the dead top of the list.

Zach inhaled long and deep, hoping to calm the madness brewing inside of him. When his breathing returned to normal he tipped his head back against the wall and looked around the room.

Sela was gone.

"Care to tell me what that was about?" Luke Hathaway stood staring at the wall of computer monitors in the Recovery Project's warehouse headquarters. With one hand balanced against the console, he hovered. He was good at hovering.

Ever since Recovery had lost its government funding and disbanded as a quasi-official agency, it operated even deeper undercover. When Rod Lehman had disappeared—the man who'd handpicked the Recovery members and set the group's mission—Luke had stepped up to serve as de facto leader.

A serious injury to his shoulder made him a possible vulnerability to his fellow agents in the field. Not that he regretted the move that took away partial use of his arm since it happened while saving his wife, Claire, the love of his life and the person who now bankrolled the Recovery Project.

But the change in financing meant no more fancy downtown Washington, D.C., offices with the fake cover of an antiques salvage operation. No more formal law-enforcement assistance. No more protection if they stepped too close to the line. That was all long gone. Now they had a nondescript beige warehouse by the southwest waterfront. It didn't look like much but the technology inside rivaled that of any government intelligence agency thanks to Adam's technical expertise.

Being in command, taking the lead but often staying behind when the bullets started flying, let Luke play a major role without his unwanted disability causing a problem for his team. It also allowed him to focus and make sure the group's original mission never changed. They specialized in finding missing people, those who were taken against their will and those who disappeared on purpose. Locating Rod, now presumed dead, was their main job and a constant source of frustration.

They were experts, could find almost anyone, and they couldn't find this one man who meant so much.

Since they'd just come off a series of cases uncovering corruption in the Witness Security Program—WitSec—that left several of the program participants dead in a cash-for-information scheme by the very officials charged with protecting them, the Recovery agents were all exhausted. They were supposed to be taking a short break to regroup and figure out what role Trevor Walters, the very rich, very connected and very dirty owner of Orion Industries, played in the WitSec murders. And if he had a partner. Which meant Adam and Zach shouldn't be handling an operation, and certainly shouldn't being doing so without Luke's involvement.

The only reason Luke knew to get there this morning was his emergency alarm went off when the building's tracking devices started humming. That meant either Adam was working instead of sleeping with his new girlfriend Maddie in the loft above the team's workspace or someone had broken in. Either way, Luke had to move. He left his house in the capable hands of fellow team member Caleb Mattern, who was also in charge of watching over Claire and Caleb's new wife, Avery. They were two women determined to help even if it meant danger, which made protecting them an even bigger challenge. But Caleb was up to the task.

Skipping his usual morning coffee and a few extra hours in bed with his pregnant wife made Luke more than a little frustrated. Things would only get worse in a few minutes when the caffeine headache kicked in.

"I'll ask again. This obviously isn't a drill since I

didn't schedule one, so what is Zach doing?" This time Luke loomed behind Adam, making sure he couldn't move his chair without slamming into either the desk in front of him or Luke behind him.

"You sure you want to know?"

"Details."

When Adam tried to spin around this time, Luke stepped back. Adam's lack of eye contact told Luke most of what he needed to know.

"Someone grabbed Trevor's assistant," Adam said.

"Sela Andrews?"

"That's the one."

"Where is she now?"

"With Zach."

Luke blew out a long breath. "Okay, and where is he?"

Adam glanced over his shoulder at the monitor. "Western Maryland. He hasn't checked in since he left the car to get her, but his watch is on. I can hear everything."

"It's bad?"

"It's not good, but Zach has it under control." Adam cleared his throat. "For now."

"Get out there. I'll take care of the communications on this end and watch over Maddie." When Adam didn't move, Luke motioned for him to get up.

"I might not get there in time," Adam said.

"Go. Use back roads. Borrow a helicopter if you have to. Move in fast and keep talking so I know where you are."

Adam went to the weapons cabinet and typed in the

security code. He loaded up with three guns, a knife and a bag of small explosives and headed for the door. He turned back right as the metal closure to the attached garage slid open. "Hey, Luke?"

Luke didn't look up from the monitors and their focus on the darkness around Zach's car. "Yeah?"

"Sorry we hid this one from you."

Luke understood. The drive to rescue was ingrained in the men he fought beside. So was the need to find Rod and have an answer, whatever it was.

Other than Rod, the only person known to have information on the WitSec scam—the side job Rod was working on when he disappeared—was Trevor Walters. The one person close to Trevor was Sela. That made her a priority.

Luke nodded. "Later Zach can give us all an explanation of why he was close enough to Sela to watch her get kidnapped."

"About that—"

"Get the woman out alive and figure out who tried to snatch her and why. We'll handle the rest once she's safe."

"Thanks."

"Just get there." Luke made the statement to the silent room, but he knew Adam understood. One second too late and Zach would be a dead man.

Chapter Three

Sela raced into the dense woods off to the right of the cabin, wishing the sun would just rise already and shed some light on her path. Her thin heels dug into mud, her ankles twisting with each step. She ran blind, having no idea of direction or what she would do if she managed to reach anywhere else.

The humid breeze pressed against her face, stealing her last breath. She gasped, her throat grabbing for air as the smell of pine filled her head. Through watery eyes she glanced back at the dilapidated cabin.

Zach Bachman. She had a thick file on him sitting on the corner of her desk. She had one for every member of the Recovery Project. Trevor watched every move they made. He never explained why, but he did make it clear he respected the team's resources. That didn't mean he trusted them, and she followed his lead.

Sela didn't understand the benefit of keeping tabs on Zach and his fellow agents, but she did what she was told. She owed Trevor that much and now it paid off. She could identify one of the men fighting over her. She just hoped she lived long enough to turn Zach's name over to the police. Let him explain what he was doing with Johnnie. So long as she was safe, she didn't care.

But stray thoughts kept hitting her even as she made her exit. Having Zach show up tonight made her wonder if he was one of the good guys or if he was with them. She didn't even know who "them" was or why they wanted her, but she wasn't stupid. Her employer, Orion Industries, specialized in threat management. They provided intelligence and paramilitary personnel to foreign governments and international corporations. Working for the owner made her a target.

Those awful rumors about her being more than an employee only made things worse. She hadn't understood that until she got hit in the head and kidnapped.

She couldn't afford to stick around now and try to put the pieces together. She certainly couldn't be sure Zach would win this round. At six-foot-something, he had the advantage over the guy Johnnie. The sleek muscles peeking out under Zach's black T-shirt also tilted the fight in his direction, but she wasn't taking the chance that his broad chest and lethal reputation guaranteed a win. And she most definitely couldn't be sure if he did win, he wouldn't harm her. No, there were too many risks for her to trust anyone in that cabin.

When her ankle twisted, she reached out to catch her balance and scraped her palm against rough bark. Half hiding, half leaning, she pressed her back against a tree and tried to get her bearings. She needed to find her internal compass. Figure out which way was north, or south, or any other direction that led out of there.

A sharp smack echoed through the woods as the

cabin door slammed open. A dark figure filled the entrance, but the light behind him plunged his face into shadows.

She didn't wait for another sign. Her brain flashed a message to her legs to move. She ran toward the dark lump in the distance, hoping it was a car or anything she could hide in. Twigs snagged her already ruined stockings and branches scraped against her forearms as she tried to protect her face.

She ignored everything around her—all the sounds of shifting and moving coming from the dark woods—except the path beneath her feet. She absolutely had to stay on her feet.

As soon as the thought entered her mind her right foot slid out from under her. Her upper body went into free fall. She put out her arms to lessen the impact and landed on all fours on the hard ground. Her kneecap suffered the brunt of the blow.

She heard crunching and harsh breathing behind her and looked up in time to see the branches behind her shift to the side.

"Sela, don't move!" The harsh whisper echoed around her.

Zach.

She couldn't see him, but she sensed him. Heard him. Short brown hair and a lean body that proved he had not gone soft since his days in the military. He'd found her.

She tried to climb to her feet, but he grabbed her around the waist and lifted her up as if she weighed little more than a kitchen towel. She kicked out her legs and fought him anyway.

"Stop," he ordered.

That was never going to happen. The fear pumping through her had her keyed up and ready for battle. She called him every name she could think of.

He coughed when she landed a heel in his shin. "I have parents."

She stilled. "What?"

"They're likely sitting on a sofa in Pennsylvania."

"I don't—"

"So that particular nickname you just called me doesn't apply."

"You're joking? Now?" Did he think it would calm her down? Because it did and the realization made her furious.

"Do you have a better strategy?" he asked.

"Yeah, we get out of here before Johnnie finds us." Hope skipped through her. "Unless you killed him."

"First, keep your voice down." Zach's grip loosened but not enough for her to slip away. "Second, he's very much alive. Bleeding and dumb as a stick, but alive."

For some reason, that struck her as the wrong answer. "Why?"

Zach pressed a finger against his lips. "Quiet."

She batted away his hand. "Answer me. Why didn't you just kill him and be done with it?"

"Bloodthirsty little thing, aren't you?"

"I have no idea why you showed up when you did, but I've got to get out of here." She lowered her voice when Zach scowled. "You can either help me or not, but I'm going."

When she started squirming again, he clamped her feet between his legs and trapped her arms by her sides. "You're going to hurt yourself."

"I'm going to hurt *you*." She clenched her teeth together and strained her neck. She tried to lift her arms but his iron hold settled around her again.

"Probably, but then you won't have any way out of here. Now, stop." Zach whispered his harsh command against her ear.

She froze this time. No movement at all.

"Are we leaving?"

"I'm not sure yet."

Wrong answer. "When will you be?"

"I'm still deciding the best way to proceed, but I can think of better places to spend an evening than with that guy." Zach's voice softened, but his grip sure didn't.

"What are you talking about?"

"In case you didn't notice, the creature in that cabin wants you dead or, at the very least, plans to take you to someone who does."

"Do you know who?"

"No. I made up the boss thing to get entrance and buy some time."

So he wasn't one of them. She relaxed a bit, until she felt a tug on her skirt. When Zach bent over and tunneled a hand up her hemline, she froze. "If you're not one of the bad guys, what are you doing?"

"Just a sec." He kept working, his fingers pulling and twisting. "I have to take care of it now."

"What is the 'it' exactly?" The staccato sound of her breathing filled her ears. She hovered right on the edge of panic. If she could keep her wits, she might be able to land a kick on the side of his head. But she had to stop shaking first.

"This."

She thought he pointed to her thigh. "You've seen a woman's legs before."

"Once or twice." His hand kept moving then he looked up. "Why are you humming?"

The buzzing sound in her ears stopped. "Am I?"

"You did that in the garage, too. Must be a nervous habit."

Rage swelled in her brain. "You were there and didn't stop that creature from taking me?"

"There was no time."

Fury flooded through her, wiping out the shakes and every other feeling except anger. "You could have shot him."

"I like the way you think."

"Why didn't you?"

"Stay still." He reached into his pocket and pulled out a knife. With a click, a blade appeared.

So he was a bad guy, after all.

No way would she be a victim. Not anymore.

She smacked her fists against his shoulders. "I won't let you hurt me."

"Not one for the obvious, are you?" Zach kept one arm banded around her waist and his opposite hand held the knife as he ducked his head to fend off her blows.

She punched him harder. "The obvious is you want me dead."

He grabbed one of her hands. "For the record, I want you very much alive."

At his words she stopped fighting. "I don't understand."

"A branch is caught in your skirt. I'm trying to figure out if it penetrated skin." He sliced through the hem and held up a sharp stick. "See? Looks like you have a cut but nothing needing stitches."

"Oh." She hadn't even felt it.

All the confusion and pain and terror of the last few hours slammed into her, leaving her bones weary and her mind blank. Men were after her and she didn't know why. A guy she didn't trust held her and for some reason his closeness made her feel safe. None of it made sense.

"I was thinking of something more along the lines of 'Why, thank you, Zach,' because you know exactly who I am and who I work for, right?" He stood and stared down at her.

"Yes."

"I'm assuming that's why you aren't kicking up an even bigger fuss."

She let her shoulders slump. "Sort of."

"Yeah, well, you're welcome." He glanced toward the cabin. "Any chance you know Johnnie or who sent him?"

"Of course not."

"Then I still have to figure out how to get you out of this mess and what's really happening here."

She breathed in nice and deep, trying to feed oxygen

to her brain. "Call my boss or the police—anyone—and get us help."

"I'm actually trying to be quiet and not say anything that would accidentally give our location away to Johnnie there. You could take a hint and keep your voice down." Zach barely made a sound as he spoke.

He put a few inches between them but kept a firm grip on her elbow. The only part of her that didn't throb in pain.

"Time to go," he said.

"Where?"

"We'll figure that out later." He glanced back at the cabin. "We need to move."

They took two steps before the sound of gunfire rang through the woods. Air whooshed around her as Zach shoved her behind the nearest tree and covered her body with his.

"Johnnie?" she asked.

Zach's heated breath grazed her cheek, but his gaze stayed focused on the cabin. "I'd hate to think someone else showed up to the party."

She pushed against his broad shoulders to get his attention. "What is he shooting at us with?"

Zach frowned at her. "A gun. What do you think?"

She thought about punching him. "Why didn't you take his weapon?"

Johnnie kept screaming out her name. Every now and then he'd add a threat or switch the words around to be as profane as possible, but the message didn't change. Johnnie wanted them back.

"I did. But I didn't think he'd have the brains to hide

another weapon in the cabin." Zach wiped his forehead on his sleeve. "Score one for Johnnie."

"I thought you were some superspy type."

"That's a terrible description and no." Zach glanced at his watch and clicked a few buttons. "Okay. Change of plans."

He'd totally lost her. "Which means?"

"We're going back inside the cabin."

"Are you kidding?" He put a hand over her mouth as she started to shriek. She mumbled the rest of her question into his palm.

"I almost never kid."

She shrugged off his hand and tried unsuccessfully to step back but ran right her foot into the tree behind her. "Absolutely not."

Zach exhaled. "The only way out of here is through Johnnie."

"You came in a car. We'll leave in it." She grabbed Zach's shirt in an effort to reason with him. Looking into those greenish-blue eyes, she tried to will him to help her.

"We have to know who Johnnie is working for. At the very least, we need to make sure he doesn't call in reinforcements."

"You know people."

"True, and I've sent an emergency signal to them. They're on the way, but I don't know who Johnnie's boss is. I only know his name because he was dumb enough to use his own car when he kidnapped you." Zach hauled her to his side with a gentle tug.

"What does any of that have to do with getting out of here?"

"Right now my biggest worry is the people who will come for you next if we don't stop Johnnie and get some answers."

The words sent a new bolt of fear spinning through her. "I'll go to Trevor."

"I'm not sure that's safer."

"He's my boss."

"Maybe, but for now you're stuck with me." Zach marched her back to the cabin, balancing her weight against him as her shoes slipped.

She tried to postpone the inevitable but nothing worked. Her so-called rescuer was leading her right back to the beast, dragging her along in big steps and not giving her a choice. A few more feet and he'd hand her off and she'd know for sure just which side Zach was on. And she feared it wasn't hers.

"Zach, please."

"Follow my lead." He gave his order right as he dumped her at the base of the front steps. Right in front of Johnnie.

"You're a dead man." The harsh yellow porch light made Johnnie's pale face look jaundiced.

Sela couldn't remember ever seeing a person look that color. Not a live one, anyway.

Zach treated Johnnie like a speck of dirt. "Get out of my way."

"No way, man," Johnnie snarled, his eyes glazed over and his ripped and bloody clothing hung from his body. "I don't know who you are, but she stays with me."

"Who paid you to start thinking, Johnnie?"

Sela closed her eyes as her head began to spin. This couldn't be happening. The scene reminded her of two rabid dogs fighting over a piece of meat. First time in her life she saw herself as nothing more than food.

"The boss needs some information from her. That means I gotta hurt her bad."

"If you touch me, I'll kill you," she said.

"I got the gun, so I make the rules." Johnnie thumped the barrel against his chest as he sneered at Zach. "What do you say to that?"

Zach nodded, the movement slow and deliberate. "Okay, Johnnie."

"Stop talking like we know each other. We don't."

"Right. You make the rules."

A new wave of panic washed over her. "Zach, what are you—"

"It will be fine." His grip on her arm loosened.

"Don't you dare give me over to this guy. I will hunt you down and…" Something. She'd do something nasty and violent if Zach abandoned her now.

Her hands clutched at his shirt. She'd pull out every one of his chest hairs and then rip through him if she had to in order to make her point. When Zach stared at her with cold eyes, a bolt of fear crashed through her. Then she heard it. A whisper so low she thought she slipped into a dream. "Trust me."

Trust me? At Zach's toneless murmur she wanted to run, to scream for help. To do all the things that would seal her death.

Before she could argue, he set her to the side, steadying her with one hand. He made one last command, this one in a much stronger and louder voice for Johnnie to hear. "Stay. I'm not chasing you around the woods again, woman."

"That's right," Johnnie said.

Zach turned back to Johnnie. "Okay, my arms are free. No weapons. No bullets. You want to see who's in charge of the lady now?"

Johnnie nodded in Zach's general direction. "Where's your gun and the one you took from me? I want that back."

"Lost mine and yours is still in the cabin."

She hoped that wasn't true. In fact, she counted on it being a lie from Zach meant to throw the attacker off. Johnnie was just dumb enough and out of it enough to believe him.

Johnnie's gaze clouded. "No way, man."

Or not. She inhaled, hoping Zach had another plan since this one seemed doomed to fail.

"If I had a weapon it would be aimed at you right now," Zach said.

"I've seen you fight with fists. That was bad enough." Johnnie looked from Zach to her and back again. Sweat formed in the dirty creases on his forehead as desperation sparked behind his cold eyes.

"Thought you wanted to battle man-to-man," Zach said.

"I have a better idea." Johnnie pointed the gun at her. "Come here."

"Never going to happen." The hours of being bait

ended now. She was done being a pawn in this screwed-up game.

Johnnie spit a wad of blood onto the porch. "Now, lady."

Zach held out an arm and blocked her path. "Stay right where you are."

"You don't want to fight me," Johnnie said.

Zach held up his hands in surrender. "You're right. So, why don't you put the gun down?"

If she hadn't been watching Zach so closely she might not have seen the sharp blade peek out from the edge of his shirtsleeve.

"No deal," Johnnie said.

"I'm going to put my hands down."

"Fine, man, but I ain't dropping the gun."

"Well, hell, just don't shoot me by accident." The hard edge left Zach's voice, as if he were joking with a friend instead of staring down the barrel of a gun with an idiot attached to the other end. "I don't know any woman worth being shot for, do you?"

Johnnie hesitated, then let out a cackling laugh. Within seconds the obscene sound turned to a wheezing cough. "Only good for one thing."

Zach frowned at the other man. "You okay?"

"Let's hope not," she mumbled under her breath.

Johnnie tried to suck in air. "I think you broke my rib."

Zach whistled through clenched teeth. "Man, I start fighting and something takes over."

"You're insane when you throw punches."

"You have no idea." Zach lowered his hands at the same time Johnnie eased his grip on the gun.

As soon as Johnnie pointed the barrel toward the cracked wooden porch, Zach brought his arm down in an arc and sent the knife slicing through the air. The blade shot in a direct line and lodged with a sickening thud in Johnnie's shoulder.

He squealed as his gun fell to the hard floor and his body slammed into the porch post. In a flurry of profanity, he slipped to the ground. A crimson stain seeped from around the new wound.

Sela wanted to run, but her legs wouldn't move. Too much of her energy went to keep from screaming. She didn't have anything left in that second for an escape.

Zach kicked Johnnie's gun, sending it sliding off the edge of the porch. In the next breath, Zach snatched his supposedly lost gun from behind his back and aimed it at Johnnie. "Don't you ever threaten her again."

Johnnie heaved and coughed. "Whatcha want with her?"

"That's my business."

Wrong, it was her business. And not knowing provided the perfect reason to get the hell out of there. She inched back toward the wall and started to do just that. If she could keep Zach focused on Johnnie, she had a chance to escape. To where, she had no idea. Preferably somewhere without a gun.

"Don't even think about it, Sela."

She froze at the sound of Zach's husky voice. "What?"

"Whatever it is you're planning in that head of yours."

"I didn't… I…"

"You're coming inside with me."

Wrong, wrong, wrong. She'd tried playing along. Maybe begging would work. "Let me go, Zach, please."

"This isn't a bargain." He grabbed her elbow. "We have some things to talk about."

She tried to break his hold but wasn't any more successful this time than the last. "You're going to regret this."

"I have no doubt."

Chapter Four

Trevor Walters paced the length of his office from the door to the windows towering behind his desk. With every step, the memory of the call played in his mind. The toneless whisper of the male voice and the threat.

It is over. All ends will be tied.

That was three weeks ago. Three weeks after the WitSec mess screamed to a halt and he reached a tenuous new peace agreement with the Recovery Project. Even now he waited for the windows to implode and the agents to storm in with guns at the ready.

Except for the soft hum of the computers set up on the credenza, the executive suite remained quiet. The main offices one floor down buzzed with the usual decreased level of weekend-morning activity. His was an around-the-clock business. He set strategies in place for businesses that sent employees into dangerous locations. He could handle the worst, often did.

Ever since Recovery agent Adam Wright breached the office's security and infiltrated Trevor's office with weapons aimed at his head, no one got up on the private elevator and his floor without his express approval.

He hadn't granted it to anyone except the two guards stationed by the elevator. Visitors or Orion employees trying to get in would need the security codes and the guts to get through men with guns.

Except for Sela. She worked on the floor. She belonged there.

Being at work on a Sunday wasn't unusual for him, but he was there on this Sunday, at this predawn hour, because she called with an emergency. Since starting as his assistant almost a year before, she'd been consistent. His most loyal supporter. As his life fell apart and his ex-wife raged in the newspapers about the need to limit his access to their son, Sela stood strong.

She ignored the whispered comments about sleeping with the boss and concentrated on her work. In return, he piled even more responsibility on her. She was the only one who knew about the extent of his surveillance on the Recovery agents. She coordinated the information he gathered and kept her mouth shut.

She was a valued assistant. And she was running late today. That never happened. From the wobble in her voice, the rushed words over the phone a few hours earlier, he knew something had happened.

Now she didn't answer her home phone or cell. Her desk chair was empty and she didn't leave a message after the one begging him to come to the office immediately.

She was missing.

Sela, with her integral knowledge of his dealings, could very well be a loose end to be tied. Her death would guarantee her silence and his.

Trevor didn't waste another minute. He slipped between his desk and his chair. Typing in the code to his bottom right drawer, he opened the small safe and pulled out the gun. He brushed his fingers over the cool metal. The weapon felt good in his hands, solid.

He ran a multi-million-dollar business, but he wasn't the type to just sit behind a desk. He'd taken the time to learn how to shoot. And he would use those skills to protect Sela. He just hoped he wasn't too late.

SELA SAT ON THE COUCH and rubbed her knee. The chair barricading the door ensured she couldn't get out before Zach could get to her.

But that didn't stop her from talking. "Zach, you're not listening to me."

He stopped counting the number of times she said that sentence. Pretty soon he'd need a calculator to do the addition. "That's right."

"You have a chance here."

"Uh-huh. A chance." He rattled around the kitchen drawers until he found rope sturdy enough to hold Johnnie once he regained consciousness.

Zach checked for weapons. Also looked for a phone and evidence of a partner or a real boss. This time.

Seeing Sela run into the dark woods had rocked his concentration enough to make him screw up that big. In his rush to get to her before anyone else could grab her, he'd failed to watch his flank. He'd let Johnnie launch an offensive strike that could have taken Sela out, anyway.

Zach wanted to kick his own butt for missing the obvious.

And Sela wanted to talk him to death.

Somewhere in the past few minutes she'd decided he was one of the bad guys and was set on redeeming him. She kept up her motivational speech from her seat on the couch. "You're on a road to nowhere."

"Actually, I'm not sure what town we're in."

"What?"

"Nowhere is probably ten miles to our east." He wrapped the rope around Johnnie's legs and arms and pulled tight, making a perfect military knot.

While Sela lobbied her position, Zach did what he could to stop the bleeding on Johnnie's shoulder and chest. He added a gag, just in case Johnnie woke up yelling. As a final protection, Zach dragged the injured man across the floor and locked him in the tiny bathroom. No need to see him if he wasn't conscious to answer questions.

"He could die in there," she pointed out when Zach returned to stand in front of her at the couch.

"I'm rarely that lucky."

"Zach."

Hearing her say his name, with her big brown eyes all soft and hopeful, made him feel something. He couldn't put a name to the feeling but an unsettling sense of lightness poured over him. Rather than deal with that unknown, he focused on his other problem. Getting them out of there alive.

She had other ideas. "You're still not listening to me."

"I'm trying very hard not to, but you sure are not making it easy."

Her chin raised and a deep red stained her cheeks. He'd seen that look many times since he'd started watching her. There was something else, too. Her eyes, glazed with distress and fear, told a different story.

He felt like a piece of crap for not seeing it sooner. She had to be in pain. A bruise marked her soft skin. A torn blouse. Swollen knee. Seeing her hurt made him sick.

He didn't dwell on the sympathy but there it was, pulsing in the dark spot in the back of his mind. "Let me see your leg and check that cut."

She braced her hands against the sofa cushions. "I'm fine."

And ticked off. The beautiful woman with the model face and stripper body definitely was not happy.

Leaning down on one knee, he met her face-to-face. "Don't be a hero, Sela. You're injured."

"So are you. Johnnie landed a punch or two."

Zach pretended to be offended. "Is that a comment on my manhood?"

"Take it however you want."

"Men are sensitive about stuff like that, you know."

"Johnnie needs medical attention."

She knew how to kill a decent try at chitchat. "Like I care."

"You'll care if he's dead and you're on trial for his murder."

"You're the one who wanted to know why I didn't shoot him earlier."

"That was adrenaline talking."

"Well, Johnnie is lucky I didn't kill him." Zach sent a disgusted look in the direction of the locked bathroom. "I might yet."

"You wouldn't."

He scoffed. "Why would you think that?"

"You're not a killer."

The matter-of-fact way she said it stunned him. "Sounds as if you've had a change of heart about me."

When he leaned forward, she pulled back, forcing her bruised body deeper into the couch cushions and away from him. "Not that much."

"I'm trying to help."

"If you want to help, drive me home. Call Trevor. Do whatever you need to do so I can talk to the police." Her voice dropped. "Or just leave me alone."

Hearing her talk about Trevor—her boss and suspected lover—made Zach's jaw clench tight. "Not going to happen."

"Which part?"

"Any part." Especially the part where he left her alone.

He slipped his hands under the hem of her skirt. Ignoring her slapping hands and yelp of surprise, he skimmed what was left of her tattered stockings down her legs and ripped them from around her injured knee.

"What are you doing?" she asked in a voice more breathy than firm.

Yeah, what was he doing? More bad timing. This time his.

Concentrating on her bruise instead of the silky feel

of her skin proved impossible. It hit him out of nowhere and without warning. He wanted her.

He knew she was messed up with Trevor, a man Zach despised. She was likely sleeping with the guy, caught up in whatever garbage Trevor had going. But no matter how hard Zach tried to make that matter, it didn't. After all those days of watching her, studying her, Sela's image played in his mind, and he could not figure out a way to shake her loose.

He swore under his breath, berating his lack of control. She'd been hurt and mistreated. She'd probably just experienced the worst three hours of her life. All he could think about was bunching that businesslike skirt around her waist.

He *had* become an animal.

"Well?" she asked.

He swallowed down a lump of unwanted attraction. "It's not broken, just badly bruised and a bit cut up."

"Tell me why," she said.

"I'm not a medical expert, but a bruise has something to do with blood pooling under the skin."

"Not that." Her face didn't show any emotion. "Why did you save me from Johnnie only to drag me back here and continue to keep me against my will?"

Because reinforcements were on the way. Zach knew if he had any hope of finding out the person behind Sela's kidnapping, he needed to stay put. Knowing Adam was heading there right now made holding the position a bit easier, but Zach still hated being out in the open in a situation he couldn't control.

"It's not over," Zach said.

"Did anyone ever tell you that you tend to talk in half sentences?"

"Once or twice." With as gentle a touch as possible, he probed the area around her knee. Sela winced and squirmed but stayed quiet. He knew she feared letting him see her weakness. He admired that.

"Call the police."

"Your knee will feel better in a minute." He unbuttoned his shirt and yanked it off his shoulders. His sore ribs protested, but it was more important to keep Sela's knee immobilized and stable than to worry about his battered insides.

He stripped down to his white undershirt and folded his dark shirt into a long, slim bandage. "I know it's not clean but it should work okay."

Sela's body turned to marble. The sudden change caught his attention. His gaze shot up to meet hers. Her seething anger evaporated and in its place came surprise.

"What's wrong with you?" he asked.

She blinked several times. "Nothing."

His eyes narrowed. "Tell me."

When she continued to stare over his shoulder with her mouth clamped shut, he gave up and wrapped her knee. "Better?"

"You keep ignoring my questions. What are we going to do now?" she asked, this time her voice a bit less shaky.

"We're not going to do anything."

She leaned against the cushions. "We're just going

to sit here?" If her bulging eyes were any indication, she didn't like the idea.

"For a second." He glanced at his watch.

"Care to tell me why?"

"I need to keep Johnnie covered so he doesn't call in more guys to pick up where he failed. I also want him dragged in and questioned."

"What does that have to do with us sitting here?"

"I can't do it alone. We're waiting for reinforcements."

"You mean more Recovery agents." Her mouth twisted as if she'd just smelled spoiled milk.

"You don't sound too happy about that."

"No."

"What did we ever do to you?"

"Adam Wright threatened to kill me."

The news surprised Zach…and it didn't. When Adam had thought Trevor kidnapped Maddie, Adam's woman, he'd stormed into Orion with guns loaded. Sela had tried to get in the way, which was one of the things Zach both admired and upset him about her. Loyalty was an impressive commodity. Too bad sleeping with Trevor blew every positive attribute apart.

Zach cleared his throat as he blinked the disturbing idea from his mind. "I'm thinking you're exaggerating."

"He held a gun on me."

"Well, yeah, that sounds like him." Zach could imagine that happening. "If it makes you feel better, I'll force him to apologize the second he gets here."

"When will that be?"

Zach stared at his watch one more time. "Good question."

"Could you narrow it down?"

"My guess is about five minutes from now."

Chapter Five

Luke glanced up as the warehouse security door slid open. He didn't reach for his gun because he knew the visitor's identity. Watched him enter the security codes and drive into the garage. Holden Price belonged there. He was part of the team.

"It's not even dawn yet." Holden yawned as he talked.

"Blame Zach and Adam."

"I intend to." Holden flipped the chair next to Luke backward and sank down into it with his elbows resting on the back.

"Where's Mia?" Luke thought about Holden's fiancée and her refusal to get married until they had a final answer on the WitSec matter, and he couldn't help but smile. That woman had guts. And her mandate drove poor Holden insane.

"She's with Caleb. Dropped her off a few minutes ago at your house. She whined the entire drive."

"Sounds like she's not a morning person, either."

"True, but I still think Caleb got the worst end of this. He's got your five-months-pregnant wife and two other women to watch over, none of whom are happy about being dumped on him and all of whom insist they don't need a bodyguard. And, between us, they could be right. I wouldn't want to be on the wrong side of any of them."

"Why do you think I got out of there so fast?"

"You're not alone." Luke and Holden shared a laugh before Holden glanced at the monitor in front of him. "So, where are we?"

"There's a disaster brewing in Maryland."

"I can assume my dear Adam is behind it." Both men turned around at the sound of Maddie's voice. She wore sweats and a frown that made it clear what she thought about the Sunday-morning job.

"Good morning," Luke said.

Her frown deepened. "Not so far."

Holden stood long enough to kiss Maddie on the cheek. "How are you doing?"

"Enjoying not being chased after but still not happy about waking up alone." She hitched her chin at the screens. "Where is he?"

"Helping Zach," Holden said.

She shook her head. "I knew they were cooking up something."

Luke respected a great many things about Maddie. She had given up everything to testify against a brutal ex-boyfriend with a drug-dealing business. The move landed her in witness protection, which should have meant security for her but didn't. A cash-for-information scam hatched by WitSec officials had put her and other participants in danger. A scam involving

Trevor's brother and a host of government officials, including the guy from the Justice Department whose division decided who got into the program and who didn't.

Maddie Timmons was one of those people in danger. The very professionals she'd entrusted with her safety had sold her whereabouts and new identity to someone who wanted her dead. She was only alive now because she'd refused to give up and had trusted Adam with her safety.

In the end, when given the choice of reentering the program or throwing in with Recovery, she had picked them. That meant living in the warehouse temporarily until Adam could find them the right place to live and the prosecution could finalize the new charges against her ex-boyfriend, this time for attempted murder, but Maddie rarely complained. Only Adam's secrecy could set her off, and Luke knew the feeling.

"How'd you know they were working on something?" Luke asked.

"Lots of changing the subject when I walked into the room. The sort of thing they think is secretive but is really just annoying." She waved her hand in dismissal. "Are they safe?"

"Should be."

The corner of her mouth kicked up in a smile. "That's what I like about you, Luke. You don't sugarcoat."

"Sorry."

Holden clapped, drawing their attention back to the problem at hand. "What do you need me to do?"

Luke no longer had a choice. One of their own could

be involved in this mess. Not any of the members of the team, but a tangential factor—Vince Ritter, Rod's original partner back in the U.S. Marshals Service.

Together, Vince and Rod had worked on placements in witness protection before they retired and Rod started Recovery. They had been the initial contacts for all the witnesses who'd ended up dead, and for Maddie, the only one in the scam to make it out alive. It made Luke sick to think they'd called Vince in for help while he may have been the mastermind behind it all.

But the alternative was even worse. When men came to take out Maddie a few weeks back, the team floated the idea that Rod was still alive and on the run. That he was the man behind the information-for-cash scheme in WitSec that had cost so many lives and put the program in the bull's-eye of congressmen who worried the corruption had weakened the program's effectiveness.

"I want you to pay a visit to Vince," Luke told Holden. Then he nodded toward the communication equipment. "Go in hot so we can record his comments."

"Interesting," Maddie mumbled as she made her way over to the coffeemaker.

Luke knew Maddie didn't trust Vince. As an outsider, she questioned Vince's role from the start and refused to share information in his presence. "If he is behind the WitSec conspiracy, then he likely has a hand in trying to kidnap Sela."

"Trevor's assistant?" Maddie asked.

"Zach stepped into the middle of the plot and now has her."

Holden's low whistle split through the silent room. "Damn."

"Right. So, if you're on top of Vince, you'll be able to assess and control while everything is unfolding. We still don't know where his loyalties lie, and I don't want to find out the hard way."

"Which is?" Maddie asked.

"Over Sela's dead body."

Holden broke the sharp silence. "And what excuse do I use for stopping by his house at dawn?"

"That's your problem."

Holden snorted. "Thanks, Luke. That's nice of you."

"What can I do?" Maddie asked as she poured them all a round of coffee.

Luke knew the answer but went for it, anyway. "I suppose you wouldn't consider letting Holden drop you off at my house so Caleb can watch over you."

"Not a chance."

"Just until the WitSec stuff is behind us."

"Still no."

"Figured." Luke knew what Adam would want him to do but that didn't mean Luke was going to pull rank on Maddie. Let Adam handle that thankless job. Luke had enough on his hands with Claire wanting to jump into the middle of the investigation.

Maddie pointed at the 3-D map on the screen. "Now, show me where Adam is so I can go from being worried to furious."

Luke couldn't help but smile at that one. "It's amazing how well you fit in around here."

She snorted. "We'll see if Adam feels that way when he gets back."

Holden barked out a laugh. "I look forward to hearing that fight."

SELA EYED THE CHAIR balanced under the doorknob before switching her gaze to Zach's broad back. He stood at the dirty sink and washed his hands, acting as if she didn't pose any threat to him, that he could turn away and not risk her running.

He had more than fifty pounds on her. She knew from his file he was thirty-one, which made him about six years older. Stronger, bigger and faster. Yeah, getting away from him was not going to be easy. And she wasn't even sure she wanted to.

She should have been furious. He admitted to following her and watching the attack in the garage. He spewed all sorts of allegations about Trevor. Still, when the bullets flew and Johnnie went mad, Zach stayed and fought by her side. No one had ever done that for her before.

In two steps he was in front of her, staring down at the makeshift bandage around her knee that he'd fashioned from his shirt. Her breathing still hadn't returned to normal after his impromptu striptease. She'd see that impressive chest every time she closed her eyes for a month.

Right now she couldn't see anything because he was right on top of her. The man did like to crowd her. Even now one of his legs balanced against her good knee.

"What?" she asked, almost dreading the answer.

"You're humming again."

The music in her head cut off. "I was?"

He smiled. "Anyone ever tell you that you could sing?"

"No."

"Good."

"Why is that good?"

"Hate to think about someone lying to you."

Amazing how fast he went from attractive to annoying. "You're hysterical."

His smile faded as his hand went to his gun. "Stay there."

"Where would I go?"

He stalked to the door, so quiet for a man his size. With his back against it, he checked his watch. "Damn."

Seeing him on the edge made her stomach flop. "What is it now?"

"Slide off the couch and to the floor. Be careful not to put too much weight on that injured knee."

A snide response to his order died in her throat when she saw a tic in his check and stiffness across his shoulders. He'd shifted into soldier mode. That meant trouble lurked outside somewhere. More trouble.

She dropped down, invisible knives cutting through her knee as she went. Dragging her body on her elbows, she slipped behind the sofa. The cushions wouldn't stop a bullet, but she didn't exactly have a list of good options to choose from.

"We've got company," Zach whispered.

"Someone from your team?"

"Wouldn't tell you to hide if that were the case." His gaze skipped to her before returning to his watch.

She was two seconds away from taking the thing off of him. "Is the time really that important right now?"

"There's a camera on my car."

"Well, of course there is."

He ignored her comeback. "Using that and this watch I can see outside."

No wonder Trevor respected this team. They seemed to have a contingency for everything. "Sounds reasonable. I guess."

"You know how to use a gun?"

She blinked at the quick change of topic. "Yes."

"Really?"

"Trevor insisted all Orion employees take weapons training." Trevor viewed it as a personal safety issue. When she'd stalled in starting her lessons he took her to the range himself and wouldn't let her leave until she tried it.

Zach stared at her, as if weighing the chance of her shooting him in the back. "I see movement up the driveway. Looks like a man advancing toward the house."

"Johnnie's boss."

"More like his firepower. I'm betting he's coming to take Johnnie out, get rid of any evidence and take you to the real person behind all of this. Only question is how many are coming."

A wave of dizziness crashed over her. She'd gone from one bad situation to another. From an untenable work situation to a dangerous one. All she'd wanted was a simple desk job and no drama.

"Give me a gun." When he shot her a scowl, she held out her hand and tried again. "You can trust me."

He could. She couldn't explain and certainly didn't want to analyze it, but she suddenly knew he was the right guy to get her through the next few minutes. Only a dumb woman ran from a protector, so she was done doing that. She didn't know what to call someone who was silly enough to shoot her rescuer.

"They're probably looking to end this before dawn," he said.

"How do you know?"

"It's what I'd do. You want the protection of darkness, and that means moving in," he said. "Our job is to stall until Adam gets here."

"What can I do?" She stood as she asked the question.

"You should keep your weight off that leg for a while."

"I'd rather have an injured leg than be dead." She moved her hand, holding it toward him in a not-so-subtle hint.

"Smart choice." He bent down and pulled a smaller gun out of a holster on his ankle. "For you."

Mistrust and concern warred in his eyes. Finally, he motioned her closer and handed over the weapon. He kept a rock-solid grip on the handle even after she grabbed it.

"Zach?"

"Right." He dropped his hand.

"Where's Adam?"

"A few minutes out."

"Meaning?"

"We're on our own." Zach pulled her toward the couch as anxiety zinged around the room.

"I was afraid of that."

With her pinned to his side, he tipped the furniture over until it formed an upside down V. Using his hip, he shoved it closer to the door, then ducked behind it. In two seconds, and with only one available hand, he built a barricade and tucked her on the safer side of it.

"Keep your head down," he said.

"Definitely."

"Unless I say otherwise, as I move, you move." His voice had dropped to a rough whisper. He checked his watch again, then said, "One is on the porch." He delivered the bad news, then put a finger over his lips.

Sharp cracks, like the sound of bursting balloons, ripped through the quiet morning. A second later, the wood on the front door shredded. As her mind jumbled, Zach dove on top of her.

Pressed flat against the hard floor, her teeth rattling, he covered her. His hands protected her head and his gun dug into her hip. With each muffled blast his body bucked and her hurt knee slammed down, sending new ripples of pain through her.

She heard a high-pitched scream as the drywall chipped from the wall behind them in time to the *rat-a-tat-tat* of the bullets. Kitchen cabinets pockmarked with bullet holes flew open. The bathroom door took the biggest hit. The door splintered, wiping out the loud thumping sound inside.

Through the hair covering her eyes, she saw flashes

of light outside the cabin and watched the holes in the door grow and connect until nothing stood between them and the morning humidity rolling in from the outside.

"Stay here." One second, Zach's weight pressed against her hard enough to indent the floor. The next he was gone.

In a fluid move, part sleek and part feral, he stepped around the side of the couch. Curled and moving, he dove through the air, aiming chest-high with guns in both hands, as he unloaded.

The burst of gunfire burned through her ears and echoed through every inch of her body. She covered her head but the sound continued to vibrate all around her. It wiped out the screaming. It wasn't until the noise stopped that she realized it came from her.

Curled in a ball, she tried to hide as much of her body as possible. She rocked and hummed until the deadly silence hit her. Careful not to draw attention, she slowly unrolled, peeking her head over the torn cushions. The place looked like someone shook it until everything fell apart. The punishing firefight left little standing and a smell of metal in the air.

She stumbled to her good knee just as a figure stepped through the ragged hole in what used to be the door. He was clad all in black, with a helmet and huge gun, and she didn't see an inch of skin.

"Sela Andrews?" The voice was monotone. Unrecognizable.

Her legs wouldn't work. Neither would her voice.

The man motioned with his gun for her to get up. "Where is he?"

She knew the "he" meant Zach. She did a quick glance around the room at the overturned furniture and smashed walls. In the small space near the kitchen area, she saw legs. Zach's legs. Unmoving and sprawled at an odd angle, he lay facedown with one hand thrown out to the side with a gun right next to his thumb.

Dead. He—they, maybe—killed Zach.

Every nerve inside her screamed. Already unsteady on her feet, her knees turned to liquid. She grabbed onto the edge of the couch to keep from falling down.

The gunman walked over to Zach and kicked the gun away. As it spun to a thump against the wall, she felt the last of her hope die. A pained emptiness filled her. Every muscle went limp.

Then she felt it. The heavy weight of the gun in her right hand.

She never thought she'd be able to kill another person.

She'd been wrong.

As the gunman lifted his weapon, she raised her arm. If she was going to die today, she'd go out fighting. She took aim just as he spun around to face her. Her hand shook and her heart pounded hard enough to move her entire body.

The second before she squeezed the trigger Zach came up off the floor in one fluid swoosh. Without any sound, he jumped to his feet and slammed his shoulder into the gunman, sending his shot high and wide behind her. Off balance, the two fell into the wall. The intruder shifted his gun until the muzzle passed by Zach's ear but Zach ducked, elbowing the other man over and over until he bent double.

But the guy didn't give up. He barreled into Zach's stomach with a roar, sending him flying backward, off his feet at an odd angle into the small counter. Grunts and curses accompanied each punch. The attacker's gun bobbled between them, then fell to the floor. Each reached for it, the guy having the edge, until Zach tramped his foot down on the barrel. Knocking a forearm under the guy's chin, Zach sent the other man's head snapping back.

Sela followed the wrestling figures with her weapon. Violent shaking made aiming downright impossible, but she held on until her arms ached from the pressure.

The man took another swipe for his weapon but Zach was all over him. A second gun appeared out of nowhere. Sela had forgotten Zach had taken one off Johnnie, that Zach even had another weapon until he whipped it up and aimed it right at the other guy's head. "Do not move."

The churning in her stomach refused to ease. No matter how many signals her brain sent to her arms, she couldn't lower her weapon or hold her trembling muscles still. Zach was her first line of defense but she wasn't giving up her position of strength.

The attacker moved in slow motion. With his hands up, he stood, his attention never wavering from Zach or the weapon in her hands.

"Forehead and hands against the wall," Zach said. "One sound and you're dead."

Instead of scaring her, Zach's icy tone stopped the room from spinning underneath her. She saw the blood on his lower lip and a frightening wildness in his eyes. "Are you okay?"

He didn't even spare her a glance. His stance didn't waver. Gun up, legs apart and totally in control.

"Just give me the girl and you can leave," the attacker said.

"Hands up."

When the guy didn't immediately obey, her gaze traveled between the men. From experience she knew this was the moment. The point where she became road-kill. Zach owed her nothing.

"She stays with me," he said.

The air rushed out of her lungs. The relief was so great she felt her stomach drop to her knees.

After a few deep breaths she regained her voice. "What do we—"

In the space of one word to the next, the man started moving. His fingers slid into his vest as his body spun around. Before she could yell a warning, a bang exploded through the room.

One shot. Right into the man's forehead. He dropped, mouth open and eyes wide with shock.

She choked out a word, more of a babble than anything comprehensible. That fast, Zach was in front of her, his gaze searching her face and a firm hand on her arm. "Sela?"

She reached up to touch the harsh lines around his mouth. "You killed him."

"It was either him or us."

She understood. Zach thought she was complaining, judging. Neither thought ever entered her mind.

He lowered his gun and dipped his head low and close to hers. His breath tickled against her cheek. "I didn't have a choice."

"Zach."

"These are split-second decisions. I can't stop to ask your opinion or give a warning."

"I know."

"You think of it as spy stuff, but it's really about assessing a situation and beating the odds."

"Zach!"

He frowned. "Yeah?"

"Thank you."

Chapter Six

"He's on the move." Luke cursed as he said it.

"Who?"

Lost in thought and staring at a series of computer monitors, Luke forgot Maddie was in the warehouse. That she lived there while they worked on a way to keep her safe. Right now she sat behind him at the conference table, typing away on a secure laptop.

He smiled at her over his shoulder. "Didn't mean to bother you."

"It takes a lot to do that. Years of running makes a woman pretty tough."

"No kidding."

She tapped her pen against her open palm a few times before trying again. "What has you so jumpy?"

"Trevor."

She leaned back in her chair. "Ah, the root of all problems."

"Sure feels that way."

"What's the issue this time?"

"He's at Sela's apartment building."

"Interesting." Putting the pen down, Maddie stood

and leaned over Luke's shoulder. "Looks a bit nervous, doesn't he?"

She had a good eye. The usually calm Trevor paced outside the front door of the building where his assistant lived with a phone attached to his ear. After a few seconds, he shoved the phone in his pocket and held on to the door handle for a second before it opened.

"Guess someone let him in," she said.

"Probably had someone working on getting the access code." Luke pointed to the camera aimed at Sela's apartment door. "I'm betting this is where he's headed."

In seconds Trevor appeared on that screen. He walked off the elevator, straight for Sela's place. He didn't have to call for help this time. He had the key and didn't hesitate to use it.

"I never had a key to my boss's house, did you?"

"Actually, I'm the boss." And he had a key to every team member's residence and a few more to the safe houses they used now and then. Over the past few months Holden, Caleb and Adam had all lost their homes. Even though they never complained, it was Luke's biggest regret.

"Think Trevor and Sela are..." Luke swallowed the word on his tongue. This was Maddie, not one of the guys.

She laughed at him. "A thing?"

"Yeah."

"Does it matter?"

"I think it might to Zach."

She sat down hard in the open seat next to him. "This could get—"

"Interesting?"

"I was going to say problematic."

Luke had another word for it: *disastrous*.

SHE SHOULD HAVE BEEN terrified or at least disgusted. Instead, Sela stood there, her warm palm against Zach's chin. She looked at him like he'd handed her the world.

This was not good at all. He had to put a stop to all the touching before he joined in and all common sense left the room. "There could be more men out there."

"I know."

He slipped his hand over hers. In his head he said it was to keep her fingers from skipping over his skin that way, but other parts of him knew better. "We can't—"

She cut him off by placing her lips over his. Soft and light, she touched her mouth to the corner of his in a light kiss, then pulled back again.

Blood roared in his ears, muffling everything else, including the warning signal firing off in his brain. It took all of his control to keep from wrapping his arms around her and treating her to a real kiss, one that would wipe away all the fear and pain of the past few hours.

But he couldn't. She belonged to someone else. Walking down that road, no matter how much he wanted it, spelled danger.

She treated him to a sweet smile. "I'm grateful for your reflexes."

He let his hand linger on her arm a few seconds longer before setting her away from him. "It's my job."

All traces of a smile fled. "I'm not your assignment."

"Maybe not, but I took responsibility for you the minute I stepped into that parking garage." He bent down and picked up the other man's gun. With a quick pat, he conducted a search for more and felt a surge of disappointment when he didn't find a cell phone, even though mercenary types rarely carried them.

"Well." She tugged on the bottom of her tattered shirt. "That's decent of you."

He ignored her mumbled words. No matter how much being close to her heated his blood, he would not act on it. Could not.

The only answer was to keep his head on the task in front of him. Stay in the moment. Focus on the job. Anything else could get them both killed.

"Stay behind the couch while I check out the area," he said.

When he stepped around her, she grabbed his arm. "You can't go out there alone."

"Why?"

"You really have to ask?"

"I'm just looking outside. Not going far. Won't leave." He didn't know if she'd be happy or ticked off at that last part, but he added it anyway.

"Have you forgotten about the guys with the guns?"

Zach lifted his hands and let her see the weapons he held. "So far we've seen one guy and he's not a problem anymore." Zach spared the dead guy a glance. "Besides, if someone else is out there, they aren't the only ones who are armed."

"I'm serious."

So was he, but he didn't bother to point that out.

"And I'm not leaving your side," she added.

It was as if she wanted to torture him. This close he could smell her hair and get lost in the dark chocolate of her eyes. "You'll be fine."

"I will if I'm next to you." She lifted her chin. "No arguments."

The dare wasn't all that subtle. She intended to stay plastered to him, regardless of how she had his temperature spiking. The mix of unspent adrenaline and a beautiful woman was a dangerous thing.

"Are you in charge now?" he asked.

"When it comes to my life? Yes." She slipped around until she was half beside him, half behind him.

The death grip on the back of his shirt clued him in to the panic welling inside her. The vulnerability got to him. She might act tough and date a powerful man, but she was human.

He'd rather think of her as a hot secretary who earned her job on her back. Thinking of her as a worthy partner, as a woman instead of another man's plaything, made her real. And that scared the crap out of him.

The familiar sound filled his head. "You're humming again."

The noise cut off. "Sorry."

"No problem." Heck, he was starting to like it.

With one last glance at the car camera on his watch, he turned to the problems inside the cabin and headed for the bathroom. Her choke hold on his shirt stopped him after two steps. "Uh…what are you doing?"

"The door is that way." She pointed outside.

"I'm checking on Johnnie."

She eased up, but Zach knew he'd have fingernail imprints on his upper back for a week after this. "I was hoping we could forget about him."

"Did until two seconds ago." Using his foot, Zach pushed the broken door open. It slid two inches before it hit against something solid. The slick red streak across the exposed tiles told the rest of the story. "Damn."

"He awake?"

"No."

"I don't know how anyone could sleep through all of that."

Sleeping was the least of good ole Johnnie's problems. "Uh-huh."

"Why did the bullets sound different?"

The question caused Zach to tear his gaze away from Johnnie's dead open eyes. "What?"

"Yours were louder."

Zach stared at her, wondering how they'd gone from fighting bad guys to idle conversation. It wasn't until he felt the slight tremor running through her hands and against his skin that he had an explanation for the odd chatter.

Reaction. After all the violence, the dead bodies dropping at her feet and the guns aimed at her head, her insides were likely imploding. Most people would have splintered, been curled up on the floor crying. Not Sela. She was on her feet.

She just kept on surprising him. Kept on showing she was more than blonde and beautiful.

He pulled the bathroom door shut again. "Silencer."

"What?"

He showed her the attacker's gun again. Pointing to the end, he indicated the device. "This one has a silencer."

"But I heard the sounds of the shots."

"Silencers don't really silence all sound. It's not like in the movies."

She held the gun, balanced it in her hands. "I see."

"Disappointed?"

"A little."

Footsteps pounded on the wooden porch right before a dark figure flew through the door. The blur screamed to get down as he tripped over the couch and made a diving roll to the side.

Zach had his gun up and aimed before the guy hit the floor. It took another breath before he could ease his finger off the trigger.

With an arm around her shoulders, Zach dragged Sela down beside him. "Don't move."

"It's me. Don't shoot!" Adam yelled his warning as he backed against the wall in a crouch.

After the initial flurry, silence pulsed around them. Zach pushed up to his knees and looked across the small room. Adam sat exactly where he landed. His chest rose and fell in a rapid beat.

"You're late."

"Hey, I drove fast," Adam said.

Zach forced his hand to relax. A twitchy finger on the trigger could lead to trouble, and they had enough of that already. "Nice entrance."

"You know me. I'm all about the show."

"Stats?"

"We've got one alive out there at sniper range and closing in." Adam glanced at his watch, then around the room. "You take out this one?"

"Yeah, he was likely your guy's partner. Plus there's another one in the bathroom."

"You've been busy, but could you do me a favor?"

Zach didn't miss the amusement that had moved into his friend's voice. "What?"

"Could you ask your friend to lower her weapon?"

Zach turned around and saw Sela, elbows balanced on the couch with the attacker's gun in her hands. She looked ready and quite able to kill.

"You can't shoot Adam."

"Thanks for that." Adam glanced at his watch one more time.

Zach put his hand over Sela's and lowered the weapon, but his attention centered on his partner. "See anything?"

"The camera on the car gives us limited access only."

"Not to butt in, but why don't we get into one of your cars and get out of here?" She shifted her weight until one knee rested on the floor and the injured leg stretched out in front of her.

"The man with the gun trained on the front of this house is pretty determined to make sure we never get to the car," Adam said. "Getting around him without being seen was tough, but he surely saw me nosedive through what used to be the front door."

Sela's gaze traveled the room before landing on Adam. "Just how did you get past him?"

Adam smiled. "I'm good."

"And modest." Zach sized up the situation and decided Adam sat in the safest place. Out of the range from the open door and snug in a corner. They could cover Sela there. "Go sit with Adam," he told her.

She shrugged out of Zach's light hold. "I'm fine here."

"Adam?" Zach waved his gun in Adam's direction. "Apologize."

"Excuse me?"

"You threatened her a few weeks back. I promised I'd make you apologize." Zach ignored the shocked stares from Sela and Adam.

She shook her head. "I never said—"

"I threatened Trevor, not her," Adam said at the same time.

"Look." Zach held up his hands, trying to get everyone to calm down and keep quiet. "She needs to trust us. She doesn't trust you."

Adam's eyebrow rose. "Does she trust you?"

"Yes," Sela said.

Her answer filled Zach with an immense sense of satisfaction. "Apparently."

"We need a distraction. I'll draw his fire and you can get her to the car, then—"

Zach started shaking his head before Adam finished the sentence. "No way. Maddie will have my hide if anything happens to you."

The window above the kitchen sink shattered, ending the argument. Glass rained down, pelting the floor. The room broke into action. Adam jumped to his feet. Zach stepped in front of Sela and tried to force her closer to the floor and behind what was left of the couch.

"He's coming around front."

As soon as the words left Adam's mouth, Zach started moving. He'd made it two steps to the side before a gun appeared in the front door and shots rang out. They passed close enough for Zach to feel the movement of air by his shoulder, then they sprayed across the inside of the cabin.

By the time the figure slid into the room, the three of them were ducking for cover. The offensive strike gave the attacker the brief window of advantage to get within inches of Sela.

"Zach!" Her scream bounced off the walls.

The man reached for her over the couch but caught nothing but air. Zach pressed her head down as he straddled her body. If anyone was getting shot or going down, it would be him. Since the close contact put the gun right at his forehead, that was a greater possibility than he'd hoped.

"The girl for you." The raspy voice didn't offer another option.

"No." Zach had already turned down that offer. And he had a secret weapon who was right now creeping up from behind with his gun loaded.

"I have a different suggestion." Adam pressed his gun against the man's upper back. "You drop the gun and we let you live."

The man picked the third choice. He swung around, firing as he went. Adam jumped to the side as he shot back, but it was Zach's bullet, placed right in the thin seam on his neck between all the protective padding, that took the guy down.

Deep breaths filled the air as the layer of smoke floated to the ceiling. "That was close," Adam said.

Sela pressed her body against Zach's side, her fingers curled around his forearm and her body vibrating with fear. The simple touch calmed the blood speeding through him but did nothing for his anger. He swore under his breath.

"What's wrong?" she asked.

"He's dead."

"Isn't that good?" Her voice carried a what's-wrong-with-you squeakiness as it rose an extra octave.

Adam shook his head. "No."

Zach wanted to hit something. Preferably revive one of the idiots in the room, question them and then start punching. "Definitely not."

"Why?"

Zach glanced at Adam and saw the answer on his face. The same one that was on Zach's tongue. This wasn't over. They had no lead, other than Trevor.

"We wanted to question him," he said for Sela's benefit.

Adam shrugged. "I doubt he would have said anything anyway."

"Now we don't know who wants you dead," Zach said.

All of the color leeched out of her cheeks. "So, the men will keep coming."

He couldn't look at her with this one. "Yes."

Chapter Seven

Trevor braced his palms against Sela's breakfast bar. He should have insisted she move into a high-security building, a place he could control and monitor. But no way would she have agreed without a fight.

As it was, false rumors about their supposed affair pushed her to the edge of quitting more than once. Having Adam burst into the office with a gun a few weeks back only added to her stress level.

Since there were so few people he trusted, Trevor had asked her to stay on. She was trained and loyal. She never asked questions and she understood his moods. In a word, she was perfect. Never anything to him on more than a professional level, but no one believed them.

Sela heard the whispers. So had he. He ignored them. She dwelled on them.

Not that he could blame her. She was trying to build a career, to resurrect her reputation after being wrongly accused of financial wrongdoing at her last job, and find a future. He had convinced her she could do that at Orion.

And now she was missing.

His check a minute ago confirmed what he already suspected—the building's security tapes had been wiped clean from an external source. Surveillance showed her leaving her apartment, then nothing. It was as if she disappeared before hitting the elevator.

Trevor knew better. The mysterious caller had talked about tying up loose ends. He'd hoped that meant the Recovery Project agents. He sensed it included him. He never thought he'd moved Sela into the line of fire.

Now he had to figure out where to turn. His team specialized in kidnapping protocols, but this wasn't business. This was personal. Only a few groups could locate those who seemingly vanished. The best would never help him. Luke had made that clear when they brokered their informal agreement. In exchange for telling them Maddie's location when she disappeared, Luke and his team agreed any evidence in the WitSec probe that led back to him would go no further, not from Recovery. If someone else found it, Recovery wouldn't save him.

That meant Trevor was on his own.

SELA WAS SO TIRED she could drop. It was ten in the morning and the sun shone bright outside. Still, after a night of running, hiding and ducking, she didn't have any energy left.

That wasn't quite true.

When it came to Zach, she had plenty of reserves. He'd driven them through a wooded area and back into Washington, D.C. When she'd asked to go to her apartment, he'd refused, reminding her that someone out there wanted her dead. Contacting Trevor was out of the question, so she hadn't even made that request.

Now they were stationed in a small corporate studio apartment in southwest D.C. The place was as sparsely furnished as the cabin had been. It had a bedroom area and a small sitting room near the front door that consisted of a love seat and a table.

She knew the neighborhood because she could see the Potomac River and the National Mall in the distance. There was a small balcony, but Zach had locked the door. He'd also pulled the curtain and unplugged the phone. Not hard to see he was serious about the lockdown thing.

"We can get supplies tomorrow," he said as he lined up several weapons on the dresser under the mirror.

She wondered if he even had a clue what a woman would want in an emergency grocery run. She guessed she'd get a toothbrush and little else. "How long are we going to be here?"

"As long as it takes."

She leaned back with her palms against the mattress. "Is that really your answer?"

"Trite but effective."

"I need to let people know where I am."

He glanced at her in the mirror but didn't bother to turn around to face her. "Who?"

The deep scowl grabbed her attention. He seemed furious and a little rough. From the stubble on his chin to the ruffled dark hair to the cut at the corner of his mouth, he looked like a guy who'd been in a bruising fight. And he had been.

When she didn't answer, he began his cross-examination. "Your parents died years ago, one after the other, from cancer."

The man knew his Sela history. For some reason, that didn't impress her. "Yeah, I know."

"You don't have any siblings."

"True."

"From what I can tell, you focus your life on your work."

It sounded pathetic when he broke it down like that. She could walk off the face of the earth and the only person who would care was Trevor, and that was only because she kept his schedule. Had her life really become so dreary and cold?

"You must have other things to do than dissect me."

"No."

"This is my life we're talking about here."

"Hard to argue with that."

The man-of-few-words had returned. Between the clipped responses and the weapon obsession, he didn't need her to fill in the blanks. He could handle this alone.

She stood. "Continue this without me."

That fast, he whipped around to face her. "Where are you going?"

"To shower."

He nodded toward the stacks of pillows behind her. "You should sleep."

The man-is-in-charge ordering was getting a bit out of hand, but she let it pass. He'd killed for her. When a guy took that step, you cut him some slack.

But that didn't mean she'd jump when he yelled. In fact, he could stop with the raised-voice thing anytime now. "Since you asked so nicely, which you didn't, I'm not getting into bed before I wash the dirt and blood and heaven only knows what else off me."

His gaze wandered all over her. "Smart."

The skin under his heated gaze tingled and her breath hiccuped in her lungs. "What about you?"

"You'll have to be more specific."

She fought the urge to roll her eyes. "Where are you going to sleep?"

"On the couch. The floor." He shrugged. "It doesn't matter."

The man was a good two feet longer than the couch and his shoulders would hang off the side. It was a chivalrous offer but she'd prefer to have him well rested and thinking soundly. "You can have half of the be—"

"No." His voice cracked like a whip.

"Wow, you weren't cryptic there, were you?"

"Meaning?"

"I get it."

He gripped the edge of the dresser behind him. Held on tight enough to turn his knuckles white. "It's not a good idea."

"I was talking about getting some rest. Nothing else."

"If you say so."

She should be offended. Part of her was. His reaction blew well over the reasonable line. "This reaction is because you still think I'm sleeping with Trevor."

"Aren't you?"

"No."

If possible, Zach's grip tightened. "He's very close to you."

"He depends on me."

"Same thing."

"No, it's not. There is nothing between us. Never has been. Never will be." She exhaled nice and loud to let Zach know she was sick of this topic. "I believe I've mentioned that already."

"You're a very attractive woman."

"One with her own mind. I know who I'm attracted to and Trevor is not it."

"Many women are attracted to the money and power routine."

She hated the way Zach lumped her in with all other women and made generalizations about her. In one sense, she understood the conclusion he'd made. He wasn't the only one to make it. Even Trevor's now-ex-wife dropped some not-so-subtle jabs on the subject.

Still, the random show of judgment ticked her off. "Do you actually know any women?"

"Some."

"They sound lovely."

"If you're not with Trevor—"

"I'm not."

"Then what type of guy are you attracted to?"

She debated playing it safe, then thought about how close she'd come to death over the past twenty-four hours, and skipped right over the games to the truth.

"You."

SHE'D DISAPPEARED into the bathroom right after she delivered her bombshell. Must be adrenaline burn, or fear or some messed-up sense of gratitude. There was no way she meant it. No way he could let himself believe it.

Zach repeated that mantra until no other words rang in his head. He'd nearly lost his mind a dozen times since the water shut off. Imagining her in there. Thinking about her stepping out of the shower.

This was not good at all.

Steam rolled out of the room as she opened the door. Stepping out, covered head to toe in the most ill-fitting, oversize sweatpants and T-shirt he'd ever seen. Zach wondered if Adam was trying to send a message or a warning of some type when he included the clothes in the duffel bag he brought for them. If so, it wasn't working. She looked better than Zach anticipated. Face scrubbed clean and blond hair wet on her shoulders. Man's clothes or not, she was all woman.

He waited a full minute, letting his body enjoy the sight while his brain clicked back to reality. "You can't be."

She froze with a pile of dirty clothes in her arms. "What?"

"Attracted to me."

"That's what you were doing out here while I was in the shower? Waiting to finish our conversation?" She dumped the load on the dresser next to his gun.

"Yes."

"The whole time I was in there?"

"You were quick."

"The hovering thing? It's weird, Zach."

Not the first time a woman accused him of that. "Pick someone else."

She blinked a few times before her lips broke into a smile. "It doesn't work that way."

Oh, no. He could handle a lot. A sexy but off-limits woman shooting him a take-me-now look was not on the list. "It should."

She stepped right past him, headed for the bed. She dragged down the covers and climbed in. "Don't worry. I'm not going to jump on you."

"That's probably wise since I haven't showered yet." Still he stood there. He'd honed his muscles, kept his mind sharp, but when he looked at her his internal barometer for right and wrong shut down.

She pushed up on her elbows. "Are you attracted to me, Zach?"

No way was he answering that one. "Promise me you won't leave while I'm in the bathroom."

"Answer the question."

"This is an assignment."

"I'm a woman, not an assignment." This time she shifted so her arms were wrapped around her upraised knees.

He had to get in a cold shower before he went nuts. "You can sit on the toilet while I shower."

"I've never heard that line before."

Lines of nonsense filled his brain. "In the bathroom."

"I have no idea what you're talking about, but no."

"That way I can see you while I'm in the shower." He turned toward the other room. Got almost to the door.

"So, the attraction… Is it yes or no?"

He balanced his head against the door frame and prayed she would stop talking. That husky voice kept licking at him, tempting him. "Nothing is going to happen, Sela."

"Right."

"This is purely professional."

She slipped out of bed and walked across the floor, her bare feet padding against the hardwood floor. "Couldn't agree more."

"Stop talking." Before his brain could signal to stop, his hand found her elbow and he flipped her around. With her back pressed against the door and his front pressed all over her, he leaned in. "Sela."

"Yes." Her voice was breathy as her gaze wandered over his face.

The kiss stopped everything else. Every movement, every thought. Every ounce of common sense fled when his mouth covered hers. He was left hot and wanting, his hands moving over her and his breath stalling. The need for her flashed over him like a consuming fire.

When he finally lifted his head, her lips were red and puffy and a cloud had fallen over those big, dark eyes.

Her fingers traced the hollow of his neck. "That's your version of not interested?"

"Yes."

A smile came and went before she dropped her arms from around his neck. "So, now what?"

"You sit on the toilet while I shower."

"Back to that."

"Yep." He pulled her into the bathroom as he walked.

"I'm not going to run."

He stopped and stared her down. Showed her his best I-mean-business frown. "Because of the kiss?"

"No, stud. Because someone is trying to kill me."

"I like the way you think." He dug around in the duffel bag Adam brought for him and dragged out a shirt and the vest. Yeah, Adam had thought of all sorts of protection—baggy clothes for her and Kevlar for him.

"What's that?" she asked.

"Insurance."

"Do I get one?"

"You get me."

Chapter Eight

Luke hit the button to let Holden and Vince into the warehouse. No need to give Vince a sneak peek while Holden entered the security code. Trust was in short supply at the moment, and that meant even longtime allies like Vince were under suspicion.

Especially given that when Holden had gone to Vince's house he'd found Vince heading out at dawn. After a quick call between Holden and Luke, they'd decided the easiest way to watch the other man was to bring him in and keep him close.

"What's the emergency?" Vince asked, his usual calm demeanor ruffled.

Gone was the cool indifference he'd mastered during his twenty-plus years of government service. Same green eyes and athletic build but his graying hair wore the tracks from where his fingers plowed through it. If affect showed guilt, this guy was dripping with it.

Luke did a short mental count to keep from yelling. They had to keep up a pretense of sorts. "We've intercepted some communication on Trevor."

Vince's gaze darted to the monitors in front of Luke.

They showed the outside of Luke's house and Trevor's office and nothing else. "Has he started up the WitSec cash scheme again?"

Holden leaned against the top of the monitors. "He lost his assistant."

Vince's eyebrow lifted. "Lost?"

Luke didn't like making Sela more of a target than she was, but he didn't have a choice. Someone was after her. Something was happening. He feared the man in front of him, along with Trevor, played a role in all of it.

The realization made white-hot fury bubble in Luke's stomach. He'd set up the warehouse and led Vince right to them. Luke had made the decision to call Vince out of retirement and ask for some guidance in finding Rod, a move that would backfire if Vince was the key to it all.

"She's gone," Luke said. "Missing."

"Any idea where she is?"

Holden tapped on the console. "None."

"Just the usual company attrition?" Vince pulled out a conference chair and plopped down in it, as comfortable in the room as he'd always been. "She's young, right? Even in a tough economy she could have gotten a better offer. Maybe she moved on."

"Not likely." Luke answered the question, then shot a scowl in Holden's direction to get him to stop the annoying tapping.

"Then we have the worst-case scenario. Is there any reason for Trevor to get rid of her? Maybe she knows too much." Vince didn't appear particularly disturbed by the idea. He actually smiled.

The longer the conversation went on, the harder the knocking in Luke's head became. It took all of his control not to slam Vince up against the wall and force him to tell what he knew about the problem in WitSec. "We're hoping to find her first and ask her some questions."

Vince frowned. "What makes you think she'd turn on Trevor?"

"Because she either left him because she wanted out or got snatched because of her ties to him. I'd think, either way, she wouldn't be feeling too charitable toward him right now."

"No woman would," Holden said.

Vince looked back and forth between the other men. "You have someone on Trevor?"

Luke threw down the challenge. If Vince was behind the newest surge of mercenaries to cross their path, he'd have to think twice about where he sent them and when. "Always."

"Good. That's good." Vince leaned back. "What can I do to help?"

"Just filling you in. Want to keep you apprised in case you think of something that could help." It almost hurt Luke to say the words. His team didn't need anyone outside the group. That was clear to him now.

Vince clamped his lips together, as if analyzing a difficult problem. "Still nothing on Rod?"

Luke marveled at how long it took Vince to get to that question. Rod Lehman was Vince's former partner and supposed good friend. He'd been missing for what felt like forever. In Vince's position, Luke would have been camped on their doorstep demanding action every day. That's what Luke would do if a member of his team were in trouble. Hell, he didn't sleep most nights from worrying about Rod and what had happened to him.

The fact that Vince had stopped checking in on Rod made Luke's temples pound even harder. "Hasn't used his credit cards under any alias. No money movement and all the usual channels are quiet."

Vince shook his head. "This isn't looking good."

"What are you thinking?" Holden's relaxed stance was in stark contrast to his strained voice.

Vince blew out a breath. Fidgeted in his chair. Generally made a show of thinking and weighing his words. "We have to face the possibility that John Tate had Rod taken out."

John Tate, the deputy director of the Justice Department's Office of Enforcement Operations. He was the man who decided who got into witness protection, or he did until Adam killed him in a rush to rescue Maddie.

At the mention of the other man's name, Luke saw Holden's jaw clench. Luke suspected Maddie, too, was ready to explode in her quiet position hiding under the stairs. After all, Tate had been the inside man at the top of the WitSec scam that endangered and killed so many people, the female participants, the others involved in the scam, innocent bystanders and mercenaries sent to protect the scam's secrets. Tate sat back in his big government office and collected piles of cash for giving away protection participants' locations. And he'd given the order to have Maddie killed.

In Luke's view, John Tate was an easy answer on the question of Rod. Now dead, Tate couldn't name his associates or take responsibility. Without Tate, Luke didn't know if everything was truly over, but he did know Rod was still missing. "I'm not ready to go there yet."

"Don't blame you," Vince said. "Do you have anything left to review and monitor?"

Time to plant the other seed. "Yes."

Surprise flickered across Vince's face until he controlled it again. "Care to share?"

"Can't."

"What does that mean?"

"We got some information. Some private files. We're still going through them." That part wasn't a lie. Congressman David Brennan had won the seat vacated at the death of Bram Walters, Trevor's equally corrupt brother. Bram, the same man who gave Tate the needed congressional cover so Tate and his buddies could start the WitSec money-making plan and then tried to kill Holden's fiancée, Mia, when Bram decided she'd figured out the scheme. The same Bram that Holden and the rest of the team killed.

David wasn't like his former boss. As far as Luke was concerned, David could be trusted. He understood the importance of maintaining the integrity of WitSec but refused to endanger the participants further. He had handed over Tate's private files and asked Recovery to find all the players and end the WitSec killing game. They'd vowed to do just that.

The only problem, the only exception, was that in exchange for the information that led to finding Maddie, they'd agreed to leave Trevor alone. Luke didn't regret the past decision. Maddie was more important. But giving Trevor a pass grated. It also made Luke more determined than ever to find something else on the man and take away everything that mattered to him, all the money, power and prestige.

Vince held out his hand. "Let me see. I'm happy to take a look at what you have."

Luke stood and walked toward the door. "I'll call you."

It was not the most subtle move and Vince got the point. After a few seconds of hesitation, he followed the unspoken command. "Yeah, you do that."

As the door clicked shut behind Vince, Luke flipped on the monitors. "You put the tracker on his car?"

Holden snorted. "Of course."

"I hate that guy, but he's not stupid." Maddie stepped up to the table, hands on her hips. "He has to know you suspect him."

Luke knew it was a risk but one that he had to take. If Vince was dirty and guessed they knew it, he'd get sloppy. He'd move too fast and slip up.

At least, Luke hoped that was true. They all needed their lives back. Running on the edge was fine. Living there permanently was not. "He's known that for over a month. I wasn't exactly subtle when I switched the security codes and suggested he not come here without an escort."

"Yet he's not complaining about being shoved out, which is odd. I'd be demanding an explanation if I were him." Holden shook his head. "Adam has been all over Vince's records and can't find any sign of the illegal WitSec money. If Vince has it, he's not moving it or making it obvious."

Luke didn't think that was a sign of anything. Vince knew better. "Which makes him smart."

"Now what?" Maddie asked.

"Holden?" Luke turned to his friend.

"I'm on it." He grabbed his keys out of his pocket. "Adam should be here any second now that he's done the forensics at the cabin in Maryland. I'll go help Caleb on point at your house. Send over what Adam collects so Mia and I can analyze it."

Maddie watched Holden load up with weapons as she spoke to Luke. "You think Vince will attack your house? Claire?"

"I'm not taking the chance he won't."

Chapter Nine

Sela came awake with a start when Zach slapped his hand over her mouth and dragged her over him to the floor with an arm wrapped around her waist. His shoulder took the brunt of the fall and kept her from bouncing against the hardwood. With his body pressed against hers and his head turned toward the front door, her brain went into shutdown mode.

Not again.

She couldn't take another gun battle. She'd just fallen asleep for a few minutes and that was only after Zach had lain down next to her on the bed. Even with her tucked under the covers and him on top, she'd felt safe.

Not anymore.

"What is it?" She whispered her question through his fingers.

"Company." He set his hand against the floor by her cheek.

"Adam?" It was the first time she wanted to see him.

"No."

"Who else knows we're here?"

"Good question."

When Zach lifted off her, she grabbed his hand to keep him right where he was. "Where are you going?"

He shot her a you've-lost-your-mind frown. "To check it out."

"It's not safe."

"Neither is sitting here, waiting for someone to storm in."

It was hard to argue with that logic. Didn't matter, anyway, since he was up and moving. He slid a gun off the dresser and into his ankle holster. Another went into his palm. The man was ready for a firefight.

That made one of them.

"Besides, I have the vest," he said as he tapped his chest.

"That's comforting."

"Here." Something flew through the air and landed with a soft thud on the mattress.

She eyed the serrated blade of the knife. No way was she going to get close enough to a bad guy to use that. She changed her mind the next second when Zach stepped toward the door. In a shot, she grabbed the knife and crept up behind him.

He didn't even turn around. "Not good with directions, are you?"

"Call Adam."

"Already done."

The charred smell hit her the second they stepped into the sitting area. Smoke crawled up the walls and hung in the air above them.

"Cover your mouth," Zach said.

She complied before he got the order out. "What's going on?"

"Someone's smoking us out."

Fire. That was a new and completely terrifying prospect. Smoke billowed under the door as the choking scent of gasoline filled the air. It was no longer a matter of when she was going to die but how. The people who were after her wanted her gone and would do anything to make that happen.

Zach pushed them toward the balcony and threw the curtain to the side. Bright sunshine flooded the room. "We need this door open before the oxygen gets sucked out of the room."

"Why?"

"Backdraft. If we feed this thing when it's just fuel and fire, it will explode."

Since that sounded too awful to contemplate, she tried to focus on the five million other problems. Anger swept away the feelings of vulnerability and gave her something to obsess about other than their horrifying situation. "Where are the fire trucks?"

"The building alarms aren't working."

Hope left her, causing her chest to collapse and her body to double over. "Any more bad news?"

"They've likely been disabled." He coughed as he pulled the door back a few inches. Air heavy with humidity poured inside. "Wet two towels in the bathroom and crawl back in here. Keep your head down."

"Right." She rushed, ignoring every pain and fueled only by panic as she crawled. Using her armpits, she hoisted her body up to the sink and fumbled with the faucet. She didn't bother to turn the water off as she fell back to the ground.

The towels dripped as she dragged them across the floor. She winced at the thumping of her sore knee and blocked out the voice in her head screaming to get outside as fast as possible.

By the time she got back to the balcony door, smoke had engulfed the room and Zach was lying on the floor, breathing out of a small opening in the door. Mumbled voices sounded somewhere on the floor.

She started to scream for help but Zach's hand against her shoulder stopped her. "No, Sela."

"We need help."

"You need to save your voice and air. Someone will call 911." With an economy of movement, he pulled her against him, then shifted until her back was pressed against him and her mouth was pushed into the opening. "Do not go out on the balcony."

All the anxiety inside her slammed to a halt as her body went numb. "For heaven's sake, why not?"

"Sit here. Breathe in as much air as you can."

"I don't—" She stared at his retreating back as he shimmied across the room on his elbows. Watched as his broad shoulders convulsed in a fit of coughing.

He'd gone insane. Instead of getting them out, he was playing around in the closet. She had no idea if fire could fool with mental wiring in that way, but something was very wrong.

She called out to him but couldn't get her raspy voice to lift above the crackling sound in the hallway. Flames licked around the door and seeped in the small slot between the top and the ceiling. Bright orange flames spread across the beige paint.

She was going to die if she didn't get Zach moving. "Zach!"

He appeared through the gray haze, crawling low and slower with each hitch of his shoulder. "Save your voice."

She'd rather save her life. "We have to get on the balcony and flag down some help."

"That's what they want."

"Who is 'they'?"

He motioned to her hand. "Keep the towel over your mouth."

She noticed the rope around his neck. "Where did you get that?"

"It's in all safe houses. Luke's rule."

"Normally I'd say it was overkill, but…"

"He and Claire got caught in a fire once. Fire makes Luke twitchy."

"He's not alone."

"Shift over." Zach reached behind her butt and hooked one end of the rope to a lever low on the floor she hadn't even seen before he touched it. "Someone is trying to force us onto that balcony. We go, we become a target."

He kept missing the obvious. "We stay, we burn to death."

"That's why I'm heading down first."

He was a flurry of movement. Hands working and tying, testing the strength of his escape plan with a rough tug. The wet rag sat in a crumpled pile on his lap as desperate coughs escaped his chest.

She touched his chin to get his attention. "Talk to me."

"I'm going out. They'll shoot at me."

"Bad plan."

"You then have a clear road to climb down. Adam is on his way. If there is a crowd, hide in it. I'm hoping the police arrive soon and you can go there. If not, run zigzagging toward people, the road, anything that's public, Adam will find you. When he gets to you, go with him."

"And you?"

"I'll be fine."

The fire roared all around them, flames racing along the walls and ceiling as smoke filled the room. Whatever the plan, they had to do it now.

"We go together," she said.

"No." He shoved the door open even farther and crawled over her lap and onto the cement balcony. "We'll see if anyone shoots at the rope."

"Zach."

But he was gone. Just as he threw the rope, a siren from a fire engine blared to life in the distance. The inside alarms might not be working, but someone had called. Now they had to stay alive long enough for the professionals to get to them. That meant keeping Zach from doing his superman routine.

"Can you rappel?" he asked, screaming over his shoulder to her.

"No."

"I was afraid of that." He wasn't looking at her now. All of his focus centered on the ground below.

"What do you see?"

"People milling. No guns, but that doesn't mean they're not out there."

"We should wait."

"Look." He nodded toward the front door. The fire had spread, engulfing the chairs in the living room and burning in a path toward them.

Her bones shook hard enough to rattle her teeth. "I can't stay alone."

This time he looked at her. Really looked. Something in her pleading eyes got through because he held out a hand for her to join him. "We'll go over as fast as possible. I'll cover you."

Once again he was risking everything to get her out of a deadly situation. She'd argue about his rescuer complex later. Right now, she needed it. "Right."

"Stay tucked. I'll fit around you until you feel like you're going to suffocate. Deal with it and stay still."

"They won't shoot with witnesses here."

"Yeah, they will." He glanced behind her, his eyes growing wide. When she went to look, he held her chin so her focus stayed on him. "Let's go."

Half curled in a ball and aching from head to toe, she slipped her body against his, her back to his chest, his body wrapped around hers. The heat from his skin burned as hot as the fire dancing in front of her.

"I'm ready," she told him.

"You hold on."

"Count on that."

"If I'm not with you, race hand over hand down this rope until you hit the ground. Do not stop moving."

He wouldn't leave her. He would not get shot. She kept repeating the words, hoping saying them would make them true.

"Sela?"

Unable to speak from the fear pinging around inside her, she nodded.

"Here we go." He jumped backward and rolled, taking them both careening off the edge of the balcony.

The hard jerk broke her hands free from the rope. She struggled to regain her grip when she heard the screaming. The rope started to swing in a wide arc. If Zach hadn't been holding her and pulling her down, she would have fallen.

Her palms burned as they scraped against the rough rope. The world flew by as they swung through the air. His feet touched the wall and he pushed off to send them rocking again. Through it all the sirens wailed and people yelled. She had no idea what was happening. All her focus went into getting down fast.

She caught a glimpse of the grass below. It seemed so far away and got farther with every inch she slid down. Just as she vowed to get down even if it meant dangling by her teeth, the heaviness behind her disappeared. She turned in time to see Zach fall the last ten feet to the ground and roll to his stomach.

As people ran away the bangs and pops registered in her brain. Someone was shooting.

"Zach!"

He flipped over, firing into the trees at the back end

of the property close to the water. He scrambled to his knees and fired in the other direction, as well. "I've got you covered. Jump!"

But she couldn't let go. Not yet. Easing her legs apart, she slithered down a short distance closer to the ground.

"Let go," he ordered.

She forced her fingers to open as her body went into free fall. Just as her feet hit the ground and gravity took hold of her body again, Zach scooped her up. With an arm around her waist, he half carried and half dragged her toward the side of the building. Bullets pinged around them as Zach zigzagged, following his own directions. Twice she felt his body tense against her, but he didn't stop.

As they hit the corner, the fire trucks raced down the street to the front of the building. Police cars squealed to a stop and people crowded together.

"Adam?" Zach's voice stayed low as he talked into his watch.

She glanced around but couldn't find him. "Where is he?"

"Over there." Zach pointed with his gun as he steered them toward the fence enclosing the apartment grounds.

Adam stepped out of a car. Without waiting for them, he cut through the chain-link fence with a tool that reminded her of a weapon. By the time they hit the area, Adam had a hole ready and pulled her through it.

He wasn't gentle and never stopped the visual search behind them. "We got police everywhere. Get in the backseat and I'll get us out of here."

They climbed inside and slammed the door shut behind them. She glanced out the window and saw officers surrounding the building, stepping right where she had just stood. If any of them looked over they'd see the hole thirty feet away and come running.

She wasn't in the mood for another chase. "Move."

"Yes, ma'am." Instead of peeling out, Adam slowly pulled away from the curb.

Anxiety revved up inside her until she exploded. She slapped her hand against the back of the passenger seat. "Why aren't you going faster?"

"Doesn't want to draw attention." Zach panted out the words as he rested his head against the seat back.

Collapsing next to him, she took in his bloody hands, his drawn cheeks and pale skin. "Thank you."

He dropped his head to his shoulder and looked at her. "You said that before."

"You hit?" Adam's bark and steely scowl from the rearview mirror grabbed her attention.

Zach tried to shrug, then winced. "Probably."

She ran her own torn and aching hands over him, checking for blood. "Where?"

"Not sure."

She slipped her fingers through his hair and pulled back when he grimaced. "Why are you so calm?"

"Last I knew, panic didn't heal anything."

"We need to get you checked out." Adam glanced at her, then back to Zach. "Where are we going?"

"Only one choice." Zach's breathing grew harsher as his words slurred.

"I don't like it," Adam said as he turned the car around in the middle of the street.

Zach nodded as he closed his eyes. "We'll argue after we see if I'm bleeding to death."

TREVOR STOOD IN THE MIDDLE of his quiet high-floor office and stared at the grainy image in front of him. The quality was subpar since it was a still from a video, but the side view of the man in it told a huge story. He was outside of Sela's apartment and the timestamp showed it was from early this morning when Sela disappeared.

Tapping on the keys, Trevor stared at the email from the unknown sender that had delivered the image. There was nothing identifiable in the email address, but Trevor already had his experts trying to trace it. He wanted to know who else had been stationed outside of Sela's house when she was taken. The image was the important piece of information and he saved that for his eyes only.

Two words: *Zach Bachman.*

After an exhaustive search of Sela's apartment and financial records, Trevor had turned to a quick check of her friends. Since Sela was not a big social person, that avenue had not taken long. People on her apartment floor hadn't seen her. Neither had the security guards, who'd been too busy sleeping when Sela disappeared to be of any assistance. Few people seemed to even know her, which struck Trevor as odd since Sela was the friendly type.

Normally he wouldn't worry about a twentysomething employee going missing for a few hours. He didn't care what they did on their off time so long as they stayed out of trouble and got their work done while at their desks.

But this was Sela. She didn't run out on her responsibilities. She also didn't whine or worry. So when she'd called him with a problem, he knew it was genuine. That shaky voice had stayed with him every minute of the past twenty-four hours.

Now he had a lead. Zach had her. Someone else was tracking her. Trevor just wished the evidence led to a less formidable adversary. Taking on the Recovery Project was something he vowed not to do again. He was a smart man and smart men learned their lessons the first time. But he was out of options. When Zach got involved, Trevor no longer cared what he'd promised Luke.

Trevor was in the business of gathering intel and making a plan. He didn't rush in, certainly not without information. Gathering pieces and putting them together was his strong suit. Whether he had the time for that now was the question.

He refused to blame Sela. He trusted her, which either meant he'd been wrong about her from the beginning or Luke's people had moved in and taken her. Neither option relieved the tightening in Trevor's chest.

At least he had a place to look for answers. He knew where she was and who had her. Why was the question.

He planned to ask Zach Bachman that in person.

Chapter Ten

Zach sat on the warehouse's conference table and wondered what he had to do to get a minute alone with Sela. He wanted to tell her how impressed he was that she'd kept it together as everything around them had fallen apart. Again.

Most people saw fire and froze. She kept moving, didn't even balk when he threw her over the side of a building.

For what had to be the fiftieth time, he marveled at how his impression of her as blond eye candy had been so wrong. Looking through photographs and studying her history, he'd been convinced before he met her that he saw a pattern. A beautiful young woman who went from one high-powered business leader to another. She'd skipped out on her former job when she got a better offer from Trevor. She'd swooped in when his marriage fell apart and made herself invaluable.

A pretty plaything. The rumors were certainly there. Trevor's ex-wife more than hinted in custody documents that Sela was Trevor's lover. Workers at Orion loved to whisper about Sela. The image Zach put together in his mind fit with everything he'd heard. Past tense. Seeing her in action since the kidnapping had ripped that impression to shreds.

Zach knew Adam and Luke believed the old Sela story was the right one. Adam didn't even pretend to like her. As he bandaged Zach's arm, he didn't bother looking at Sela across the conference table, where she was being tended to by Maddie.

"You're lucky. It was only a graze," Adam told him. "Hit flesh and passed through."

The bullet wound stung, making his whole arm numb, but Zach didn't offer that bit of information. Last thing he needed was for Caleb, their medical guy, to come running and leave the other women vulnerable back at Luke's house. Or, worse, to bring them. They had enough to deal with without the women descending.

"Not the first time," Zach said over a wince as Adam tied the bandage.

Adam dropped a wad of bloody gauze in a bag before stripping off the gloves. "The bruise on your back will hurt more tomorrow. Ribs aren't broken, but you'll be sore."

Zach knew all about getting hit by a bullet. He'd been shot there more times than he wanted to think about. "Just happy I had the Kevlar on or I'd be in a morgue."

Sela's head shot up at Zach's comment. "That was from the climb down the wall?"

"Or the run across the lawn. I don't remember."

"Why did you bring her here?" Adam stood in front of Zach but didn't bother to whisper the question.

Sela blew out a long breath. "I'm sitting right here."

Maddie shot Adam a you're-one-step-away-from-doom look but kept wrapping a gauze strip around Sela's ragged palms. Zach saw it all.

He knew where Adam's mistrust and anger came from. There were a lot of questions about Trevor, but now wasn't the time. Sela had been injured, too. Seeing that soft skin all red and puckered on her palms hit Zach like a kick to the stomach.

Zach ignored all that and concentrated on the question. "I needed a neutral place."

From the kitchen area, where he leaned against the counter drinking coffee, Luke finally voiced his concerns. He shook his head. "I still don't understand how the safe house caught fire."

"That's the story I want to hear." Adam fitted his hands to his hips and widened his stance. The position cried out for war.

When the silence stretched out, Sela looked up, then did a double take. "Why are you looking at me?"

Maddie was less subtle. She pointed her finger in the direction of the man she supposedly loved, though she wasn't looking all that loving at the moment to Zach's way of thinking. "Adam, no. Not now."

His cheeks flushed but he didn't ease up on the battle position. "We are the only people who know about that apartment." He threw a hand out in Sela's general direction. "Us and her."

Before Zach could step in, Sela rose to her own defense. "My name is Sela."

"Someone tipped off Trevor or whoever is sending these men. I doubt it was one of us." Adam's harsh tone suggested he was not about to back down from this verbal battle.

"You're blaming me?" Sela asked. "Did you miss the part where someone tried to set me on fire?"

"Did they?"

"Hey." The word caught everyone's attention. Zach pounded the floor to make his point. "Adam, ease up."

Sela's mouth dropped open. "That's all you've got to say?"

"Men," Maddie muttered as she shook her head.

So much for thinking he adequately rose to Sela's defense. "You want something else?" he asked.

"How about sticking up for me?" She was screaming now. Actually raising her voice until it squeaked.

Zach had no idea what had her so ticked off. In his mind, he set the record straight. No more need for conversation. "I just did."

She crossed her arms over her chest. "How exactly did you do that?"

"He made his point. He wants me to lay off you." The surprise in Adam's voice had Luke and Zach staring at him.

Maddie tugged on Sela's arms until they unfolded again. "Give me your hands."

"How do you know so much about first aid?" Sela asked her.

"You learn fast when you're in witness protection and have to take care of yourself." Maddie mumbled over the tape clenched between her teeth.

Adam's eyes popped. "What are you—"

"Oh, please. She knows who I am." Maddie waved

him off. Then she peeked up at Sela. "You do, don't you?"

"Yes."

Zach had taken enough fussing, and the yelling thing needed to stop. This was the point in the conversation where he usually slipped out. Folks started arguing and he got lost. He had a hard enough time around people when everything was fine. Constant fighting made him nuts. Only this time, he was at the center of it all. And he had to hang in there to make sure Adam didn't decide to interrogate Sela.

Nothing like getting stuck between a woman and his friends. This was not a position Zach enjoyed. He preferred listening to talking. The plan had served him well in the Army. Had helped him survive through those awful months when he first came back from Afghanistan.

Six hours of bombing followed by seven days of trying to dig Holden out of a collapsed mountain cave near Khost, sometimes with his bare hands for hours straight, knowing all the time his buddies in Charlie Company were suffocating. Watching men go out on stretchers, seeing Holden emotionally broken, had taught Zach something. Close off, do the job and get out. He wished he could engage in some of that right now.

He rubbed his forehead, hoping to wipe out the flashing pain behind his eyes. "Would it be possible to have five seconds of quiet?"

Sela stopped her scowling contest with Adam to look at Zach. "Are you okay?"

"Do you care?" Adam asked.

Maddie swatted at him. "Stop it."

Sela let out a sound halfway between a growl and a scream. "Look, Adam. I get it. You don't trust me."

"Wonder why," he muttered.

"I don't know what you think I did, but I would remind you that Zach took me to that safe house. It wasn't my place. I didn't set it up. You don't see me blaming Zach or you for what happened."

Adam stopped questioning her long enough to shoot one in Zach's direction. "Did she call anyone?"

Sela threw up her hands. "Can you just not see me?"

The words ricocheted around in Zach's mind. He doubled back to Adam's question, hoping to slam the lid down on the conversation. "No."

"Any chance she's wearing a wire or—"

"I said no."

Adam sputtered. "You checked?"

"Adam, stop." Maddie threw the full weight of a glare behind her finger pointing this time. "If Sela doesn't slap you soon, I will."

Luke came to stand behind Sela's chair. "I agree. That's enough."

Zach welcomed the silence that fell over the room. When Luke threw down the gauntlet it tended to work.

"Adam, man the monitors. Maddie, take Sela upstairs and find her something to wear that doesn't smell like a tire fire." Luke looked her over from head to foot. "Let her shower while you're at it."

Sela sent a pleading look in Zach's direction, but he refused to heed it. She was safe in Maddie's hands and

Luke deserved answers. They all did. If Zach had to listen to a lecture or two to get an hour of peace, he'd do it.

Luke motioned for Zach and Adam to take seats at the table. "Explain what happened."

"The safe house didn't work," Zach said.

"I see."

The tone. The narrowed eyes. Zach knew exactly where Luke's mind had wandered and rushed to cut off the thought. "Don't."

Luke's eyebrow inched up. "You sure?"

"There's nothing there."

Adam scoffed. "I'm not buying it."

"She's Trevor's assistant. Driving her right to our door was dangerous, and you know it." Luke tapped his pen end over end against the table. "I'm thinking you had a reason."

Zach wasn't a sharer and his feelings for Sela, whatever they were, were not up for the team's dissection. "Survival."

Luke didn't ruffle. He didn't stop flipping that pen, either. "We've been able to hide our location from Trevor so far. This jeopardizes that."

"Trevor and Sela are not in contact."

"You're sure?" Adam asked.

"I've been right on top of her." Zach closed his eyes. Wrong choice of words. He regretted them the second they left his mouth.

This was why he usually kept his comments short and cryptic. Couldn't get into much trouble that way.

Luke and Adam shared a look before Adam launched

into another question, this one delivered in a deadly soft tone. "When you were in the shower?"

A man didn't have any privacy around here. "She was right there."

Luke swore. "This is a dangerous lady you're getting involved with, and don't tell me you're not involved. I have eyes. She's attractive and you're not dead."

"Your point?"

"She could mess you up. You know that, right?"

Zach didn't know he was angry until the festering red monster blew. "She's been kidnapped, hit, shot at, chased and smoked out of hiding. Not once did she panic or turn on me. She was a good partner."

Adam smacked his fist against the table. "Because she knows they are Trevor's men and that they really wouldn't hurt her. She could afford not to be worried."

But she had been terrified. Zach got that much. Every line of her body had mirrored fear as Johnnie moved in, as the gunmen caught her in their sights, as the fire raged.

"No." Zach bit the inside of his cheek as he sat back in his chair. He refused to lose what was left of his hold on his temper. "I don't see it."

Luke stopped tapping and held the pen suspended in midair. "Maybe you're too close to this one."

There it was. That damn look again. Luke and Adam glanced at each other, wearing matching blank stares, then looked away again. Zach hated the insider communication. He was an insider. In this case he knew what it meant, that they worried he'd lost his objectivity.

Never mind the fact each of them had met their women during...

Woman? Yeah, he couldn't let his mind finish the thought. Instead, he went back to the work issue. "Sela is an assignment."

Luke threw his pen down. "No, she's not."

The alarm on the console beeped, slow at first, then with manic frequency. A second later, their watches joined in. Adam shot across the floor on his roller chair.

"Now what?" Zach asked, thinking he'd had enough excitement for a week or two.

Adam typed on the keyboard until the top middle monitor closed in. "This can't be happening."

Luke stayed calm. "What?"

With one more click, a close-up of a man's face came into view. "Trevor."

"What?" Panic moved into Luke's voice this time.

"At our gate. He's standing with his hands up in the air, looking at the camera as if he's known all along where we are." Adam sneered as he said the words.

Zach's mind rebelled. They'd been so careful. The warehouse's ownership was buried under a labyrinth of paperwork and dummy corporations. Claire had made sure it would be nearly impossible to trace the location back to her. They'd all engaged in evasive maneuvers when they drove to the place every single day, just in case they were being followed. Hell, they used a system of alleys and other buildings' security systems to create a hacked pathway into the place that wouldn't show up on any GPS.

The warehouse was hard to find on purpose. And Trevor had nearly walked up and knocked on the door.

"Maddie!" Adam yelled loud enough for people in the next town to come running.

She appeared at the top of the steps. "Why are you screaming like that?"

"Where's Sela?"

Maddie hitched her thumb behind her. "Right here."

"Show me."

Maddie's face went dark. "What's wrong with you?"

Sela stepped up beside Maddie, still wearing her dirty clothes. "Here I am."

Luke motioned for Adam to get up. "Go make sure everything is okay up there."

Zach sensed Sela was in for more harassment. "I'll do it."

Luke's glare kept Zach pinned to his seat. "You don't move."

"What are you going to do?" Adam asked Luke.

Luke's mouth stretched into a fine line. "Trevor obviously knows we're here, so we're going to show him in."

Zach felt the world spinning around him, just out of his control. He'd spent years creating a way of life that ensured everything stayed within a certain comfort zone. Now this.

"Sela?" he called out.

"What?"

He didn't want to believe it, refused to process it. Yet, he had to know if she was with him or with Trevor.

Yesterday the answer would have been easy. She'd side with her boss and possible lover.

But Zach had seen the doubt in her eyes as he dropped comments about Trevor's illegal past and more men came looking for her. "This is your chance."

She glanced at Maddie then back at Zach again. "To…?"

He saw Sela wrap her fingers around the railing above. He had her attention. "Show me how grateful you are."

"What is that supposed to mean?" Luke asked.

But Sela knew. Zach could see the way her gaze darted to the right as she evaded. He'd bet she was humming.

His eyes locked on hers. "Not one word. Trevor comes in and he never knows you're here. Yes?"

She nodded. "Yes."

Adam took the stairs two at a time to get up there. "I'll see to it."

Chapter Eleven

It took another ten minutes to get Trevor inside. Luke escorted him in. Picked him up at the curb and made him wear a blindfold as they drove.

After all the security fanfare Trevor stood in front of the conference-room table, clearly outraged at his treatment, and folded the black material down from his eyes. "Was that really necessary, gentlemen?"

Zach felt a nerve on the back of his neck twitch. He hated being this close to Trevor. Worse, having the other man this close to Sela. "It was either that or shoot you for trespassing."

"Well, then, I guess I should thank you for letting me in." Trevor motioned for them to sit as if he owned the place. Luke and Zach ignored him.

"We'll stand." Zach would rather kick the other man, but he settled for hovering over him. They were in control here, no matter what Trevor believed.

Keeping with his power play, Trevor pulled out a chair and sat down. He looked Zach up and down, taking in the bandage and more than a few cuts and bruises. "What happened to you?"

"I fell down."

"How many times?" Trevor touched his finger to his nose. "And did you land in a gallon of gasoline?"

Luke took over. "You've proven your point, Trevor. You know where we are. Congratulations on your investigative skills. It only took you six months to find the deed."

He held up his hands in mock surrender. "There is no need for sarcasm. I come in peace."

"That has never been my experience," Luke said.

Trevor brushed his hand over his obviously expensive suit pants. "We have a deal."

"And I am just itching for you to break it."

Luke's disinterested tone contrasted with what Zach knew was going on inside him. Zach felt it, too. Nerves pinged and crawled. They'd spent so many days trying to catch Trevor and he'd walked right up to their door and handed himself over.

It took all of the internal strength Zach had not to rip the walls apart with his bare hands. Bruised or not, he knew he had the power to do it.

"Maybe we can talk alone…or are there other ears listening in?" Trevor made a show of looking around the place.

With each condescending word Zach's control inched closer to snapping. Sela was right there and could break away from Adam and come down the stairs. Trevor could do anything or have one of his goons stage an attack. Zach itched with the restless feel of vulnerability, even though he knew that was Trevor's goal.

Luke crossed his arms in front of him, matching

Trevor's calm demeanor. "Since you previously decided to storm my house with armed guards, I have to keep a contingent there at all times."

Trevor waved the comment off. "That's in the past."

"Maybe, but I'm getting a little tired of cleaning up the dead bodies you leave behind on your informal missions. I can only go the feds and the police so many times on a need-to-know basis before people will start thinking I don't get along well with others."

After a beat of silence, Trevor tried again. "I am not here to talk about old grudges."

"We're listening," Luke said.

The face Zach saw on the news when Trevor was donating money to charity in some big show of extravagance or giving long-winded speeches about his dead brother, the crooked congressman, dissolved in a mask of fury. No longer struggling to find carefully chosen words, Trevor let the rolling anger inside him show. "Where is she?"

So, this was a mission. He wanted Sela back. Zach leaned in, pretending he hadn't heard the question. "Excuse me?"

"Sela Andrews."

"Your girlfriend?" Luke asked.

"My assistant."

Zach didn't know what she meant to Trevor, but she sure deserved more than a toss-off description. Zach struggled to keep his hands at his sides instead of around Trevor's neck. "Did you lose her?"

"This is not a game."

When Zach went to answer, Luke held up his hand and took the lead. "Why do you think we have her?"

"I saw Zach on video at her front door."

The news stole Zach's breath. He was always so careful. Adam told him the positioning of the cameras at Sela's apartment and how to stay out of sight. Zach refused to believe he'd blown cover in order to get to Sela. He hadn't lost his edge.

"You have a tape of me?"

"You're not the only ones who know how to hide a camera. You were there. She went missing." Trevor's voice returned to his usual upper crust, condescending tone. "Where is she?"

Zach tried to wrestle his thoughts back under control. "We don't hurt women, even your women."

"She is a valued employee."

He made her sound as important as a lamp. Zach hoped his instincts were right about her and that she wasn't lying. The idea of Sela with this guy made his stomach heave.

"What's the end game here?" Luke asked.

"There have been some, shall we say, issues." Trevor stared at the ceiling as if contemplating his next words. "I need to know she is here of her own free will."

The guy acted as if he'd never sent death squads after them or had his people kill government officials who could point to him as a player in the WitSec mess. "Issues? Is that what we're calling your illegal activities?"

Trevor talked right over Zach. "She was upset the day she disappeared."

"And?" Zach asked.

Trevor locked his gaze on Zach again. "I need to know if you are the reason for that."

Luke slid over, putting his body in Trevor's line of vision. "If we see her, we'll call you."

Trevor frowned. "This is serious."

"I can see that."

"If you—" Trevor stopped, and took a deep breath, as if struggling for control. After a few seconds he continued. "She is not part of our fight."

Luke cocked his head to the side. "How deep are you in this WitSec scam?"

"We are talking about Sela."

"I thought I'd take the opportunity to talk about a topic I cared about."

Zach winced at Luke's harsh tone. Since Sela could hear every word, Zach wondered if that jab was for her benefit.

"Why would someone take her?" Zach asked Trevor.

"Like you, I engage in dangerous work."

Zach hated being compared to this guy in any way. "Try again."

Trevor didn't even blink. "She is innocent."

"I doubt that if she hangs out with you." Luke kept tweaking but Trevor would not lose his cool.

And unless Adam had put a gag in her mouth, neither did Sela. She didn't come running down the steps or scream for help. Zach had no idea what that meant.

"I will find her," Trevor said.

Zach took that as a threat but Luke just shook his head. "Not my business."

Trevor delivered that *tsk-tsk* sound he was so fond of. "I would hate to see our agreement threatened over this."

Luke matched the show of strength with some of his own. "Our deal doesn't extend to your assistant."

Trevor stood. "I want her back by tomorrow."

Like he owned her. Zach didn't think he could hate this guy more. "Good luck with that."

Trevor whistled as he glanced around. His gaze ended at Luke. "Nice place you have here, by the way. It's a good use of Claire's money, or should I say of her ex-husband's money?"

Zach saw Luke's shoulders tense and stepped in before the boss lost it. Trevor was the one guy who could push Luke too far.

"Almost as nice as your office. Adam got in there without any trouble last time. Got right up to your private office and put a gun to your forehead," Zach said.

"I have plugged some security holes since then." Trevor wiped his hands together as if he'd touched something dirty or beneath him while in the room.

"And so will we."

Trevor looked past Zach. "Tomorrow, Luke."

He shook his head. "You're talking to the wrong people."

"Maybe your WitSec contact can help you," Zach suggested.

Trevor walked right up to the huge metal door of the warehouse. He tapped on the thick slab. "I suppose I need a top-secret exit code to get out of here."

"It's tempting to knock you out and throw you in the street."

"That's the difference between us, Zach." Trevor laughed at a joke only he got. "Well, one of them."

"Enlighten me."

"I fight with my brain, not my muscles."

"I prefer to use a gun."

Trevor's smile faltered a little. "I'll keep that in mind."

"You do that."

Chapter Twelve

Adam walked down the stairs a few minutes later with Maddie and Sela behind him. "What was that about?" He called out the question to his team members below.

"A warning." Luke headed for the coffeepot and started pouring.

Sela wanted to ignore it all. Sitting up there, listening to Luke and Zach throw out innuendos and Trevor not denying them pricked at her. She wasn't naive. She knew Trevor had a dark side. Washington, D.C., was a power hub and Trevor moved in the center of it. He could be ruthless and demanding.

More than once she'd heard him on the phone, spewing out condescending barbs in that smooth tone of his. He answered his ex-wife's viciousness over the custody of their son with an ongoing stream of hate. But he'd always been fair with Sela.

Despite the rumors to the contrary, he'd never made a pass. Never even looked at her in a way that made her uncomfortable. He also ignored her former boss's attempts to ruin her name. She'd been trapped by a boss trying to save his son's reputation and got blamed for embezzlement. The company insisted firing her and not prosecuting her for something she never did was somehow a gift. They said they had evidence, though none existed. They said she deserved to be unemployed, and she had been. They took everything from her and never cared. It was about protecting who they were in the community, and if that meant destroying someone they viewed as a low-level employee, then that was fine with them.

Trevor saw through it all. He heard about the so-called evidence and discounted it. He actually listened to her side and hired her, entrusted her with top secret programs and never made her feel as if she was being tested. In her mind, that made him one of the good guys. She focused on his charity work and belief in her and blocked out everything else that conflicted with the image.

Zach, Luke and Adam—they made her see Trevor in a different light. One far less flattering. If half of what they said was true, every time she picked up a phone or started investigating a private matter for him, one that was off the company books, she put someone in danger. Possibly even Maddie.

He'd sucked Sela into a life she didn't understand or want.

She had to hold on to the railing to keep from falling down. Her legs were shaky as she hit the bottom step.

Zach was beside her in a flash. Concern showed in his eyes. "You okay?"

"Honestly? No." She made it to the conference table and slumped into a chair.

"You're not alone." Adam stood right across from her and there was nothing charitable about his dark look. His fury filled the room until the air felt heavy.

Zach shook his head as he slipped into the chair beside her. "Not now."

"It's okay." She reached out and touched his hand, comforted by his closeness.

No, on some level she deserved this. She hadn't been an active participant but she let a lot slide. All those secret meetings about Luke and Recovery. She'd been trained not to trust them, but they hadn't shown her anything but decency. Sure, Adam didn't like her. That was clear, but she knew deep down that grew out of his concern for his friend. She'd put Zach in danger at least three times since he stepped into the cabin.

She'd been bred to believe they were the bad guys, unfairly hunting Trevor because he was powerful and a potential threat to them. Now that argument didn't make any sense.

Adam didn't hold back when he speared her with his piercing green eyes. "Before you stumbled into our lives, Trevor didn't know where our office was and didn't know the address of that safe house. After a few hours with you, Zach's been shot and our team has been infiltrated. Do you see a pattern?"

"I get that you don't like me."

Luke shoved a coffee mug in front of Adam and took over. "Trust, Sela. It's an issue of trust."

Something in his softer delivery made her want to open up. The way Zach squeezed her hand helped, too.

"I didn't tip anyone off. I didn't even know about the safe house until I was sitting in it."

"We'll leave." In typical Zach fashion, he delivered the bombshell, then stopped talking. Didn't explain or elaborate.

"What?" Sela and Luke asked at the same time.

Then everyone started yelling.

Zach simply raised his hand and the chatter stopped. "Look, I don't know what Trevor was trying to prove by coming here. I can't tell you what he really wants, except that for him to show his hand like that means Sela is important to him."

When this subject came up, she didn't want anyone touching her. She folded her hands together on the table. "I told you—"

"Professionally." Zach lowered his voice and leaned in close, his breath brushing against her ear. "I know you're not sleeping with him."

"How?" Adam asked in his usual booming voice.

Maddie elbowed him. "You are so far out of line."

"I'm concerned."

Zach held up both hands this time. "I just know, okay?"

Sela didn't like where the conversation had gone. She wasn't too fond of the way Zach ended it, either. He made it sound as if they were together when right now she didn't know what they were. She just knew being linked to men based on nothing more than her being a woman was starting to get old.

But the comment must have satisfied Adam. He nodded in response. "Fine."

Luke poured what had to be the fourth cup of coffee she'd seen him drink since she got there. "What are you getting at with this plan?"

Zach blew out a long breath, as if waiting until he had everyone's attention before continuing. "Trevor was obnoxious today but off his game. I think he knows Sela is in danger and that his work put her there. For some reason, he cares about her safety and his role in it and is trying to fix the damage."

"But you don't think he's behind the kidnapping?" Luke asked.

"He wouldn't hurt me." Sela wasn't sure of much but she felt confident in this.

"Do you know that for sure?" Adam asked, this time without the kick of anger in his voice.

Zach's hand found her knee under the table. The warm touch sent a surge of inner strength through her. "I have to believe it."

Luke emptied his cup with one long gulp. "So, what's your plan here, Zach?"

"I take her into hiding."

Adam and Maddie leaned against the counter, neither of them looking all that impressed with Zach's new strategy. With a quick glance, Maddie gave Adam a nod and he started talking. "Not sure that's a great idea, man. Last time you tried that you got burned out."

A chill ran through Sela. She used to think she wanted an apartment with a fireplace. Now she didn't even want to see a grill. That burning stink would stick with her forever. "I have to admit I'm not loving the idea, either."

"We're not going to a safe house or any place that can be traced to any one of us."

"Then it doesn't sound safe." Maddie leaned into Adam and he slipped his arm around her shoulders. "As someone who's been on the run and is even now in hiding, I don't recommend it."

Zach held up his hands and looked around the warehouse. "Are we safe anywhere?"

Sela didn't know the answer to that, but one thing was clear. They were doing an awful lot of plotting about her life without consulting her. She understood Zach's tendency to make a plan in his head and execute it without filling her in, but this was too much.

The I-lead-you-follow thing wasn't working for her this time. "Do I get a say?"

Zach's eyebrow rose at her sharp tone. "Which would be?"

"I go to the police. Take you guys out of this. They can question Trevor… Why are you shaking your head?" Zach wasn't alone. They all were. Even Maddie screwed up her lips and joined in.

Luke shrugged. "He's a powerful guy."

No wonder Trevor did so well. He even had these guys, these amazing men who could protect and defend better than any movie hero, believing his hype. She knew because she'd seen it over and over again. "He's not above the law."

"He thinks he is," Adam said.

"Sela." Maddie slipped away from Adam and moved to the chair in front of Sela. "I know you see him as some sort of savior but he's a bad guy. He is wrapped up in a scheme that almost got me killed. All I was doing was living my life in witness protection. Gunmen came for me."

Sela had a hard time arguing with Maddie. She was so tough. Such a force of nature. "You think Trevor sent them?"

Adam rested his hands on Maddie's shoulders. "Maybe not, but he was part of the conspiracy. He is connected to people, through his business and through the information he's collected. People who have a vested interest in keeping him happy and his reputation clean."

Sela pointed out the obivious, her strongest argument. "But I'm still alive."

"What's your point?" There was no judgment in Zach's tone, only interest.

"He could have killed me at any time." Sela looked around, willing them to get it. "Don't you understand? I was the one asking for help yesterday. I called him for a meeting because I knew someone was following me. Someone got to me before I could get to Trevor."

Adam stared at her for a second before turning to Luke. "The other player."

With that, all of the tension in the room disappeared. It was as if someone had popped a balloon and all the anger deflated. She didn't know if switching topics away from Trevor did it or if they finally believed her. Either way, she was relieved. From the way Zach squeezed her thigh, she assumed he felt it, too.

"Who is this player?" she asked.

Zach leaned back and threw his good arm across the back of her chair. "We're not sure."

"Trevor ever talk with you about this?" Luke filled his cup and finished off the pot when Maddie slid a cup in his direction.

"About you guys, yes. All the time. About Vince and how he wasn't convinced Rod was dead, yes."

Adam sighed. "Those are our two options, aren't they?"

"Sorry, babe." Maddie curled up against Adam, brushing her hand over his arm and sinking in when he returned the caresses.

Seeing the six foot–plus Adam gentled by this woman flipped a switch inside Sela. The wall of resentment building around her heart crumbled. He was human and protective of the people he loved. Sela admired that even as his attacks on her had her gritting her teeth. Watching his big hand smooth over Maddie's arm hit Sela with a punch of envy. She craved that closeness. That stability. And that's what it was. In the middle of all the chaos and danger, Adam and Maddie bickered but the heat in their eyes for each other never banked.

All of the men appeared to have that weakness for their women. She glanced at Zach, taking in his flat mouth and the dark stubble over his chin, and wondered if he would ever give his heart so freely.

"The two other people who knew about the warehouse and had access to the safe house information were Rod and Vince," Luke explained. "Either one of them could have fed the pieces to Trevor and the other members of the conspiracy, who are all now dead."

Zach snorted. "Conveniently."

"Rod and Vince had inside information on the WitSec participants. They were the handlers of the two dead women and—"

Maddie raised her hand. "Me."

So much of what they said made sense to Sela, but a few major pieces didn't. "But both Rod and Vince are one of you guys. They're insiders."

Zach shifted just enough to move the focus back to him. "Which makes this personal."

She glanced around and saw the determination in their faces, felt it pulsing through the room like a living, breathing thing. She knew she'd walked into something so much bigger than her. "You're not going to stop, are you?"

A bleakness filled Zach's eyes as a chill moved across the room. "If the trail leads to Trevor or Vince, or even Rod, we've agreed to follow it. If we don't, this could all start again."

"Apparently there's a lot of money to be made in selling out WitSec participants," Maddie said.

"Not anymore." Adam kissed Maddie's forehead. "Not on our watch."

"I THOUGHT WE SHOULD meet." Vince crossed his ankle over his opposite knee and relaxed into the chair across the desk from Trevor.

Once again Trevor found his office served as the dropping ground for weak men operating under the delusion of false power. Men who collected money from criminals and then acted as if the WitSec participants were the parasites of society. John Tate and his underling Russell Ambrose, the man who tried to kill Caleb and his ex-wife, Avery, had walked this path. Even Trevor's own brother, Bram, had gotten mixed up in the mess and forfeited his congressional office's integrity in the scam.

In quiet moments alone, Trevor had to admit his role in setting the entire plot in action. One unguarded moment he'd asked about getting rid of an ex-wife and Russell had taken the nugget and ran.

Now Vince.

As suspected, there had been an inside man at Recovery all along. It explained why the team could not just put the conspiracy down once and for all. John Tate was dead because of his hubris, but he ended up being smarter than Trevor gave him credit for. Using Vince was a smart call. Now Trevor had to figure out what game the man still insisted on playing.

Trevor cleared his throat, aiming for the right mix of disinterest and authority in his tone. "I must say, I was surprised to get your call."

"You have had some dealings with friends of mine."

Trevor had to believe Luke suspected Vince. There was no other reason for the man to keep pushing his agenda after all his partners were dead. He should slink back into the shadows and remain quiet, live off the money he'd collected and be happy.

He likely would have if it had not been for Luke and his team and their vow to find Rod, no matter the cost. Trevor decided to test his theory. "Does Luke consider you a friend?"

"Somewhat."

Trevor doubted there was even that much, which would explain the reason for the impromptu visit. "So, what can I do for you?"

"Nothing."

Not the answer he expected. "I'm not accustomed to having business meetings where I just stare at the person across the desk from me."

Vince smiled. "Do you usually prefer to have your assistant present?"

There it was. The warning shot.

Trevor tried not to move, not to let a look or move tip off his reaction to the words. The burning fury of having this rat track Sela down. "She is on vacation."

Vince unfolded and refolded his hands. "Is she?"

"Do you know something I don't?"

"Probably."

"Where is she?"

Vince chuckled. "I believe you just said vacation."

Trevor considered grabbing the gun from his desk drawer and ending this game right now. "What is it you want?"

"An understanding."

The last time Trevor engaged in this sort of conversation he ended up with Tate thinking he was in charge. Trevor had no intention of riding down that road again. "I'm listening."

"I understand you are very good at keeping confidences. Your brother used his offices to help out his friends and nearly got Claire, Luke's wife, killed." Vince hesitated, as if waiting for a swift denial or argument.

Claire's ex had nearly killed her, not Bram. Bram was well in the background on that one. But Trevor refused to give Vince the satisfaction of correcting him, of engaging in a verbal battle. Otherwise strong men often lost the battle of strategy when they talked too much. Better to listen.

Right on cue, Vince continued. "You've supplied men for some unorthodox ventures and dipped your fingers in some pretty nasty business involving John Tate and WitSec."

The man was right on the verge of admitting his role in the venture. Trevor could tell Vince wanted to brag, wanted to let the world know about this brilliance. "Would you happen to have personal knowledge about those alleged dealings, Vince?"

"I'm a retired government employee."

"Enjoying that, are you?"

The stillness and blank look disappeared. Vince fidgeted in his chair, losing that calm grace the longer he spoke. "I don't have anything to lose."

Trevor never liked that phrase. He couldn't think of a time when it was accurate. "Oh, now that's where you're wrong. We all have something to lose, be it reputation or money or our very lives."

"Eloquent. People told me that about you." Vince moved around, crossing and uncrossing his legs. "They also used the word *smart*. Are you smart, Trevor?"

"Generally." Trevor could smell it. The fear and panic. Vince was a man who kept straight until he veered so far off the path of right that he couldn't even see it anymore. Oh, he acted tough and tried to give off the illusion of control, but Trevor knew better.

"Smart men know when to stay out of the way," Vince said.

Just as predicted, the power balance had shifted. Trevor waited it out and the control came back to him. Patience. It was that easy. "That is my intention unless certain innocent parties get caught in the middle."

"Like your assistant."

"That would be a good example."

Vince stared at the ceiling for a second before resuming eye contact. "See, I've found office workers, secretaries and such tend to know a lot of information. They don't have the same pressures on them and can sometimes be made to talk."

"Not Sela."

"I wonder if that's true."

"You don't know?"

"No."

Trevor had his answer. Vince didn't have her. That meant someone else did. Trevor's mind flipped through the images from the Recovery warehouse. The smoke and injuries. Those came from fighting...from rescuing.

It seemed so obvious. She was with Zach, probably was right in the building the whole time.

"I think we want the same thing here," Vince said with more than a little menace in his voice.

Since Trevor wanted to wipe Vince off the face of the earth, Trevor doubted that was true. "And how do we go about meeting our goals?"

"When I figure that out, I'll call you."

"Until then?"

Vince stood. "Just be ready."

Trevor knew he would be.

Chapter Thirteen

With his hand against her lower back, Zach walked Sela into the open marble entryway of the stone mansion off Massachusetts Avenue. Touching her felt right. So much so that he thought about humming along with her, but he knew if he pointed out the habit again she'd stop.

Her mouth dropped open as her gaze swept over the sprawling double staircase. The off-key music faded as she threw her head back and stared at the stained-glass skylight above her.

Oversize houses were the norm for this part of the city. Ambassadors and old money mixed well here. In an area ripe with money and prestige, this house stuck out. It reigned over the rest, sitting on an incline and reaching three soaring stories into the sky.

The grounds included a guesthouse, greenhouse and separate garages for the owners' fleet of antique cars, but Sela couldn't stop gawking at the inside. "What is this place?"

"A house."

Her jaw dropped even farther. "Yours?"

"Doubt I could afford the door knocker out front."

"That makes two of us."

"It's the Hampton mansion."

"Let me be clearer." She slipped her arm through his and walked over to the elaborate table in the middle of the foyer. "How do you have a key and why are we here?"

"I'm doing some work at the house."

She skimmed her fingers over the intricate inlaid woodwork on the tabletop, outlining each differently colored square. "Shooting people?"

"I have other skills."

"Good to know."

He wasn't touching that comment. Not when his need for her lay so thick in the air. "The owners gave me a key."

"Where are they now?"

"On an ocean liner for three months."

"Must be nice."

Being trapped and unable to touch dry land for days at a time sounded like a nightmare to him. "I'm not really a water guy."

She smiled as he led her toward the door under the staircase. "That would explain why you went with Army over Navy."

"That and my dad was an Army man." He turned the knob and hit the overhead light. "We're going here."

She glanced down the steep set of steps. "Downstairs?"

"Our movements won't be seen and I have more control of the surroundings in a limited space."

"I doubt the basement is small."

"There are something like ten bedrooms and fifteen baths in this house upstairs. Trust me, I can handle and surveil the few half-finished rooms downstairs much easier." Her back heated under his palm as he guided her to the staircase.

She turned around and sized him up. "You're not lying, are you?"

"About?"

She laughed. "That was kind of a scary male response, asking me to narrow down the lie and all, but I was talking about whether you're really allowed to be in here. We're not trespassing, I'm guessing. There aren't attack dogs and a security company on the way, right?"

"I hope not."

"Uh, no." She stopped. "I know how you work now."

A heaviness lifted off his shoulders at the idea. "Oh, really?"

"You didn't answer me. I caught it that time and am not moving off the topic until you deal with it."

He put his hand over his heart in the closest thing to a pledge he could ever remember giving. "I have permission, but I don't want to draw any undue attention to the house. Hence, we go down."

"You think we were followed." She rolled her eyes. "Not sure how that's possible with the way you were driving."

"Evasive maneuvers."

"Gave me a good case of motion sickness."

"You look fine. Great, even." He tore his gaze away

from her jeans and slim shirt as he mentally thanked Maddie for the fashion loan.

"Good to know."

He pointed to the steps in front of her. "Be careful and get moving."

"Answer my other question." For a thin woman she managed to clomp as she walked down the staircase.

That was nothing compared to the sound he made. A hollow thud echoed around him every time he put his foot down. "You're safe."

She reached the bottom landing and looked around at the gray rock-lined walls and a stack of boxes blocking the way in front of them. That left an open space to the left and a narrow hallway to the right. "Not what I expected."

"It's a basement."

"It's not finished."

"Which is part of why I'm working here." The sole reason, actually. The Hamptons wanted to blow out the walls and add another usable floor to the house. Apparently, the nine thousand square feet aboveground were insufficient.

"Are you a building contractor and didn't tell me?"

"Let's just say I know my way around tools." Something about working with his hands, having the freedom of not being tied to a desk, appealed to him.

Only problem would come with hanging up his gun, and he was nowhere near ready to do that yet. Fighting bad guys gave him a purpose. Throwing in with Recovery, taking Rod's offer and running with it, let him funnel all his anger in a positive direction. Gave him a target when he desperately needed one to exorcise the ghosts that came with fighting in a war.

She dragged her fingers across the stones, then rubbed the dust on her pants. "I thought maybe there would be a pool or a bowling alley. The kind of stuff you see on TV."

"What shows are you watching?"

She pointed in both directions and went right when he nodded that way. "Tell me about this side job."

"When the government, led by Trevor's brother, disbanded the Recovery Project as a sanctioned black-ops team, we were suddenly unemployed. While Claire and Luke formulated the plan to fund Recovery as you see it now, I did some work in my specialty area."

"Which is?"

The narrow hall gave way to a large wooden door and the sitting room beyond. It lacked drywall and cement served as the floor, but one day it would be a media room. For now it was a makeshift rec room with a couch, a cooler and little else.

An electrician had run wiring, but the stark light bulbs hanging without cover from the roughed-in ceiling didn't exactly match the pristine decor upstairs. But it was fine for Zach to use when he needed breaks on the job.

"Luke is the leader. Caleb is the science and forensics guy. Holden is our strategy and tactics guy." Zach ticked off the job list on his fingers. "Adam clearly is our tech guy."

"And you?"

"I blow things up."

"Explosives?"

"Is there another way?"

"You're planning on blowing up the Hamptons' house?"

"Only that section." He pointed toward a darker area off to the side through an open doorway. "For the very expensive wine cellar they're building."

"They hired you."

She made that sound surprising but he refused to be offended. His job usually consisted of him, a wall and his tools. Having a witness, someone who could get in the way or be injured, made it hard for him to relax.

He stayed on the edge, his fingers clenching and unclenching in case he needed to do a diving catch.

"Their house manager did."

She plopped down on the couch, ignoring the dust that puffed up around her. "And where is he?"

"Taking a vacation of his own while the boss is away. He left a message that he'd check in next week."

"Until then?" She patted the seat next to her.

His legs refused to move. The muscles tightened like the ache in his chest. "The place is all ours."

When he came closer, she dipped her head to the side and stared at him. Even in the low light, her skin glowed. Blond curls swept down over her breast.

Zach knew right then he was a dead man. Ignoring her in a room full of people had proven difficult. Resisting her when alone with no one to judge or stop them turned out to be impossible.

She crossed her legs and let her foot bounce around in the air. "You still think I'm Trevor's mistress?"

"I never thought that."

She frowned. "Zach, come on."

If this were a true seduction, he'd just gloss over the truth and move on to what he wanted, but this was something else. Something deeper. She deserved to know the truth about his doubts. "I thought you were sleeping with him."

Her foot stopped moving. "Isn't that what I just said?"

"Your tag is wrong."

"Tag?" She didn't laugh, but amusement filled her voice, made it lighter.

"Since you're both adults and neither are married, you wouldn't have been a mistress. If you were sleeping with Trevor you weren't doing anything wrong."

This time she laughed. It was a rich, velvety sound that warmed the cool room. "So, you weren't judging me."

He regretted the truth now. "Well…"

"That's what I thought."

"Maybe a little. You probably haven't noticed but I'm not a big Trevor fan."

"You thought I was on the arm of a guy you hated. No matter what you call it the result is the same."

"Not really." Not in Zach's head.

Cheating took the game to a whole new level. It made a statement about her boundaries and principles. Dating a guy like Trevor just meant she had felony-bad taste in men. Zach smiled when he realized neither was an issue.

"You know a lot about this subject, do you? About marriages and mistresses?" she asked.

"Some."

"Meaning?" The flirty tilt of her head and lilt in her voice had disappeared.

"I was married once. Went off to war and she found someone else."

Sela shifted to the front of the sofa cushions, all business now. "I'm sorry."

"It happens."

She opened her mouth and then closed it again before finally speaking. "Is it that easy for you to forgive her for not sticking around?"

"Never said I forgave."

"Forgot?"

"Not so much." It ate at him back then. He used the lesson now to keep the fury banked. He never wanted to return to that place where he challenged guys to bar fights just so he could beat out the frustration festering inside him through his fists. "But that's not a bad thing. You learn."

"What about me? Do you forgive me for working on the wrong side, for believing in Trevor?"

Zach gave up his position by the door and joined her on the couch. His thigh rubbed against hers; only two thin layers of clothing separated them. "Why do you?"

"He gave me a chance."

"How?" Zach knew but he wanted the details from her.

The cumulative effect of running through two powerful bosses helped him create a mental image of her before they even met. The idea that the true circumstances differed so greatly from the story he'd woven in his mind brought both relief and frustration. If he couldn't read people and assess their files, he wasn't good for the team for much more than lighting a fire.

She fiddled with a string at the seam of the couch cushion between her legs, twisting it between her fingers, then unwinding it again. "I had trouble at my previous job. Trevor ignored the bad review and hired me, anyway."

There had to be more to it than that. "Bad review?

Her head shot up. "You don't sound surprised."

"I can pretend if you want me to."

"Ah, let me guess. You've investigated my background."

There was no need to hide it. It was part of what he did for a living, and she had to have figured that out by now. "Of course."

"I was set up."

This time she lost him. Jumped right to another topic and left him behind. "I don't understand."

"I didn't take the money."

Zach thought he might have found one more piece that didn't fit because he didn't know where she was headed with this. "The story I got is that you were sleeping with the boss and had a bad breakup when he decided to go back to his wife." It all sounded so stupid now that he knew her and tried to match the rumors to the woman in front of him. "Word was you didn't take it so well."

She dropped her head on the cushion behind her with

a groan. "If I had half as much sex as the rumors said, I would be a very tired woman."

Sex. Sela. Not a combination he was ready to tackle just yet. "So, that's a no to the relationship?"

"No, Zach. It's not true." A flurry of heat moved into her voice, then out again. "The boss's son embezzled some money. I figured it out while compiling documents for the company accountant."

"Doesn't sound like the kid was very good at it." Zach half wished Vince would slip up that way. It would make everything easier to close this case. Holden and Mia could go ahead and marry.

Zach could…well, he wasn't sure what he wanted to do. Returning to his empty apartment and holding everyone at a safe distance no longer sounded so safe. It sounded boring.

"Apparently it was easier to discredit me and bury the evidence than have the heir apparent embroiled in a scandal."

Zach realized she'd been through it. Raced from one bad work situation to another. He wasn't responsible for any of it, but that didn't stop him from wanting to wrap his arms around her and make it better. That emotion was one he neither understood nor wanted to analyze.

So, he went with the obvious. "You don't have the best luck with men."

"You can say that again."

"Once was probably enough."

She laughed. "What about you?"

"My luck with men is fine." He lifted her hand from

her lap and put it on his. They laced their fingers together.

"You know what I mean, Zach."

"I honestly don't."

She curled her legs under her as she crowded up against his side. "Are you going to be bad for me?"

"No." He said it but didn't totallty believe it.

"Does that mean you're going to keep pretending you're not attracted to me?"

He wrapped his free hand around the back of her neck and pulled her in even closer. "No, I'm done with that."

His mouth covered hers in a kiss that fired through his nerve endings. Lips against lips, his heart thundered in his chest as his tongue slid inside her mouth to taste her as he'd been wanting to do for days.

By the time he had her lying back across the couch, his hands were moving over her shirt and unbuttoning the snap on the top of her jeans. She grabbed the bottom of his shirt and drew it over his stomach. His abs twitched and sparked to life as her fingertips brushed against his skin.

He broke contact with her mouth only long enough to sit up, his legs straddling her hips, and whip his shirt off and throw it in a ball on the floor. He didn't want anything between them. With the problems at bay, he existed only to touch her.

Her hands toured his chest. Fingernails pinched his skin as her gaze devoured him in a flurry of need.

He had to have her.

He barely got the condom out of his pocket when he

heard the rasp of his zipper. She had him out and in her hands before he could find the breath to talk. Words gone and his blood set to boil, he tugged off the rest of the clothes binding them. He touched the very center of her, hot and wet, until her head flew back and her breath rocked through her.

When she was ready, her breath raspy and her eyes and mouth begging for him, he ripped open the package. His fingers failed him as he tried to unroll the condom, but hers knew what to do, sheathing him, guiding him to where he longed to be. He pressed into her before one thought passed into the next.

His last memory was of her speaking his name.

TREVOR TURNED THROUGH the long cul-de-sac and pulled up to the gate surrounding his property. He refused to use a driver and contingent of guards to get him from one place to another. He could drive and didn't need to be carried back and forth to work. To him that showed weakness. It suggested he was afraid and unprepared, and he was neither.

He tapped the button on his console to move the gate and get in, but nothing happened. Rolling down his window, he pressed the call button for his security guard. Nothing happened. No buzz. No voice on the other end. He dialed the house, listening with growing annoyance to the shrill ring.

He glanced up at the house looming at the end of the circular driveway. Light flooded the front yard and everything seemed normal. No one ran out to meet him, but those days were long gone. His ex had seen to that when she grabbed their son and all the cash she could transfer and left the house. She said he could rattle around the property until he died there, but she wasn't going to join him.

Now his life existed on a very narrow plane. Burying his brother and losing daily contact with his son narrowed his social activities to work obligations.

The security guards and housekeeper followed his schedule and tonight he'd said he'd be late and not to make dinner. But there should be movement. He'd radioed to the guards a few minutes ago to let them know he was on the way. They'd answered then. Now he couldn't raise anyone. Anxiety clenched at his gut. He reached over to his glove compartment and felt the cool metal of his gun against his fingers. Before he could grab hold, a hand shot through the open window and grabbed him by the throat with a shake. As he thrashed and banged on the horn with his elbow, the gun slipped from his fingertips and fell to the floor on the passenger's side.

With his hands raking over the gloved ones of his attacker, Trevor tried to break the death grip on his windpipe. But the pressure didn't let up. With his vision clouding, he fought to keep his eyes open and air pumping through his veins.

He blinked hard to block the enveloping mist and caught a quick glimpse of his attacker.

Vince smiled. "Consider this that call I promised."

Chapter Fourteen

This time Sela knew she was humming. A love song filled her head and she let it flow through her body.

Staring up at the rock ceiling, she tried to work up an ounce of regret. She couldn't do it.

This wasn't about gratitude or proving a point about who she loved and how. Being with Zach signaled a return to a normal life. She'd spent so much time doubting her choices and trying to figure out what responsibility she had for the problems she faced. With him she could just be.

She was all woman, beautiful and strong, and they fit.

Making love with him had meant something to her. It was freeing and empowering. She'd known him for such a short time, but being together in the most basic way, without planning or a long dating dance, made sense to her. With Zach she felt safe and cherished.

She rolled over on the hard floor and pulled the homemade throw from the couch higher up on her chest. She wore his shirt but was otherwise bare. Rubbing her legs against him wasn't helping to ward off the chill. The humid D.C. air didn't reach down here, so the cold stones acted like an ice bath splashed over her skin.

But studying him was no hardship. Dark stubble fell across his chin, adding a fierce layer to an already complex man. He kept his feelings close and his sentences short, as if protecting his heart from the tough outside world. But he was so much more than the quiet man in the corner.

He rushed in when most people would run away. He argued with her, even made mistakes in judging her past, but he reached her with the gentle touch of a man who respected women and reveled in their pleasure. All those harsh lines and rough moves faded when he ran his hands over her and pressed his mouth against hers.

She traced her fingers down his well-defined biceps and pondered how far she'd come in such a short time. No one would ever understand how a kidnapping had made her life better. There was no way to explain it or turn it around until it made sense. It didn't. All the terror should have built a wall against Zach. Instead, it opened a door to let him in.

She didn't believe in love at first sight. With the added doubts about Trevor, she barely believed in anyone right now. But she knew with a bone-deep certainty Zach was different. That his destiny wrapped around hers.

"How about sharing the blanket?" One of his eyes popped open and he stared up at her.

Her butt was almost frozen at this point, so no way

was she sharing anything but body heat. "I think we should move to the couch."

He wrinkled up his nose. "Smaller."

"Warmer."

He lifted up, balancing his upper body on his elbows. "I'd make a bad joke about keeping you warm but I'm not as young as I used to be."

"Meaning?"

He glanced down his naked body. "Need some time."

When she joined in his staring, his body twitched. "Don't think so."

With a groan, he sat up. "Man, this wasn't the best place for this. Sorry."

"I thought it was perfect."

He dropped a hard kiss on her mouth. "Why, thank you, ma'am."

"You sound like Adam."

He stared at her in mock horror. "Are you trying to kill the mood?"

"Sorry. Just an observation. You guys are alike." All strong and decent. All protective and tough. She admired their bond to one another and their fierce dedication to the women they loved. Any woman would be lucky to be enveloped in their embrace.

"It's freezing down here. Let's move around before our bones go stiff and refuse to move."

Giving Zach her best dramatic sigh, she stared up at the ceiling. "All that beautiful house up there and we're stuck underground."

He froze. "I could—"

When she saw the bowed eyebrows, she knew he'd

taken her seriously. She laid a hand against his bare leg. "I was kidding."

"You sure?"

She nodded and actually meant it. "We err on the side of safety."

"You'd make a good Recovery team member." He jumped up and held a hand down to help her to her feet.

She was too busy staring at his lean body to function. Her gaze wandered up his muscular legs to the very heat of him and then to his flat stomach. There wasn't an ounce of fat on him, and he sure wasn't shy about being naked.

She smiled, ready to praise his exercise regimen when she got a closer look at his chest. A ragged scar stretched along the top of his rib cage. Another marked his shoulder. Even now he wore the bandage from their run-and-shoot at the safe house.

His gaze followed hers. "What?"

"You're a survivor."

"I guess."

"It's ingrained."

"It's all I know."

She noticed his return to clipped sentences and knew the cause. When he felt emotionally cornered, he fell back on the false barrier that grew out of limited conversation. "In your mind people are bad, so you put them down."

"Something like that."

"What about the gray areas?"

He didn't hesitate with his response. "Don't believe in them."

For her, life was all about the gray. It was where real people lived. People were bits and pieces, some good and some bad. Believing anything else made her relationship with Trevor a sham, and she wasn't ready to go there yet. Being loyal to Zach didn't mean forgetting all the good things about Trevor. Not in her mind.

Since Zach shifted into shutdown mode, she made a swift change of subject. "Where is this wine cellar I keep hearing about?"

A smile broke across his lips. "You understand there's not actually any wine in it, right?"

"Speaking of that…" She glanced around, hoping to at least see a candy bar wrapper. Anything that pointed to food. "What about the essentials? I am talking, of course, about chips and soda."

"You don't look like you eat anything fun."

"I'll take that as a compliment."

He nodded. "It was."

"Good genes."

His gaze slipped to her breasts. "I'd say."

She snapped her fingers. "Food?"

"We're not exactly trapped down here. We can venture upstairs for a few muintes at a time so long as we're careful." He stretched, wincing as he pressed a hand to his lower back. "I'm thinking trying out a bedroom is a mistake. Too dangerous."

"You know how to treat a lady."

"I'm all about making you happy when I can, just without a bedroom at the moment." He pulled up his jeans but left them unbuttoned. "Let me show you the wine cellar."

When he held out a hand, she grabbed it. Slipping her fingers through his in an act so normal, so commonplace and real, convinced her that taking a chance on him was the right thing to do.

He stopped and tapped a finger against her nose. "Now, look impressed when you see this."

"What woman doesn't like a dirt room?"

"That's my motto." He chuckled as he flicked the switch.

A yellow light sputtered to life in the middle of the room. The dim glow lit the immediate area, but there wasn't much to see. An empty safe and a wrench in front of a hollowed-out wall. She tried to envision an impressive space with temperature-controlled compartments and bottles of expensive wine, but she didn't see it.

"I bet there's somewhere upstairs..." The words died as she focused on the stark, hollowed-cheeked look of fear on his face. "What?"

"Damn."

"Zach?"

"This can't be." He dropped her hand and stood motionless in front of the open safe door.

"What is it?"

"The explosives, the plans, my tools. Everything is gone." He turned around in the middle of the room, his arms outstretched and his mouth twisted in anger.

"Stolen?"

"Not by thieves. This is deliberate."

"I don't understand."

"We have to get out of here." He grabbed her elbow and started dragging her back across the cold floor.

She dug in her heels and forced him to turn back around to face her. Seeing the dark bleakness in his eyes, she almost regretted the move. "Tell me what's going on."

"A trap."

"You have to focus here." She put her hands on his forearms, willing him to listen. "Be clearer."

"I lock up everything. Always. Now it's all gone."

"I'm sure there's an explanation."

"Someone has it. Someone who knew how to get in and out of here without trouble."

She could almost see his instincts kick to life. He'd come up with a theory and his mind immediately went there. He was no longer listening to reason. Whatever conspiracy he saw in his head was his only focus.

She laid her palms against his cheeks, hoping her cool skin would snap him back to reality. "Listen to me."

"It was all a setup."

"What?"

"This job. The Hamptons' mansion."

She tried to follow the huge jumps he kept making. "But you said—"

"It was all meant to lure me here." He took her hands in his and stared deep into her eyes. "I know I'm right."

For some reason that was good enough for her. His senses hadn't been wrong yet. The logic didn't make sense to her, but she'd cheated death more than once in his arms and wasn't about to question whatever inner voice screamed trouble to him.

They rushed back into the outer room. Without talking and with only the sounds of her desperate pants filling the silence, they threw on their clothes. Unimportant things like socks and shoes got left behind.

Before she had her pants zipped he stalked into the main space at the base of the stairs. "Zach, wait."

She fumbled her way, tripping and limping on her sore knee after him. She crossed the threshold and caught up to him just as the door at the top of the stairs crashed open.

In a swift move refined by practice, Zach reached for his gun as a dark blur came flying down the stairs, tumbling and thumping as it hit each loud step. A man who failed to make any attempt to stop the freefall. Like a rag doll, arms flailed and shoes thudded against the rock walls. The figure fell into a boneless pile at Zach's feet before the door above slammed shut again.

"Who is it?" She really wanted to know how a person survived that type of abuse. Then she took in the dark suit and familiar shoes. "Oh, no."

"What?"

"It can't be." She tried to touch the man but Zach kept her on her feet and away from the body.

His aim at the door never wavered while he bent down to feel for a pulse. "He's alive."

Stunned relief crashed over her. "I don't know how."

Zach handed her the weapon. "Shoot if you have to."

She could barely breathe. Squeezing a trigger, even thinking, was beyond her. Still, she said, "Okay."

He slipped his hands under the man's shoulders and gently flipped him over. "Damn."

This was her worst nightmare, the one situation she hadn't predicted and secretly feared would happen once she saw him face down Luke and Zach at the warehouse.

She gazed into the face she saw every day, the one man who'd believed in her when no one else did. "Trevor."

LUKE PACED THE WAREHOUSE's small space between the kitchen counter and the conference table. He smelled trouble. The building was quiet, the streets abandoned. At Zach's last check-in a few hours ago, all was fine. It was dark now and nothing felt right.

It was a bit too perfect for his taste.

Adam stomped down the stairs, leaving Maddie walking around in the dim light above. "You're still here."

"Caleb and Holden can handle my house."

"And Claire?"

The mere mention of his wife's name made Luke smile. Even the ten minutes of nagging she'd delivered during their phone conversation made him miss her. "She's not thrilled I'm staying here for a while, but she's worried about Zach, so I get a pass."

"Then you feel it, too."

They had been together long enough that Adam didn't need to define the restless churning that started whenever the mood changed. Someone or something big was on the horizon and they both knew it. "Yeah."

"Trevor."

"That's the most obvious venue of attack, but why? He knows we'll trace this back to him after his little visit. It's like he's asking to be killed." Luke wished he would because taking the other man down would be pure pleasure.

"Maybe he thinks Sela is here and figures he can take us all out at one time."

"No, this is something else."

Adam nodded. "Someone looking to frame Trevor."

Zach hated the idea. It meant the team would actually have to step in and save Trevor. Letting the man go down for his illegal activities was one thing. Allowing him to swing over someone else's mess was not okay, not if Sela ended up in the middle as roadkill.

"This is coming from someone who knows we're here and getting closer to uncovering his role in the conspiracy." As far as Luke could tell, that left two suspects. One was too unbearable to think about, the violation so huge.

Adam reached over and tapped on the keyboard, bringing up a set of cameras. "Where is Vince?"

"Car hasn't moved and sensors say he's still inside his house." Luke knew because he'd been glued to the monitors for more than an hour.

Adam held up his hands as if waiting for permission. "I'm happy to go check."

"I'll call Holden."

"Why?"

This was the one thing Luke was sure of. If everything had reached the boiling point and the end was near, he would not have a balcony seat. He would be there, no matter the consequences. "To come here because I'm going with you."

Chapter Fifteen

Zach tried to get his mind clicking into action by counting to five. Seeing Trevor tumble headfirst down those stairs swept every other plan out of Zach's head. He hadn't counted on more bodies, more people to save. He hadn't thought the leader of this thing would take out Trevor when he came after Sela.

He sure hadn't counted on anyone finding them this fast. He now worried that the Hamptons' trip was nothing but a way to get Zach alone in the house.

Trevor groaned and Sela fell to her knees beside him. "Can you hear me?"

Zach wrestled down a lump of jealousy. She said Trevor meant nothing to her outside of work and Zach refused to doubt her. She'd shown him loyalty, given him an incredible few hours. He would not let his mind wander to the dark place where he dissected every conversation, looking for lies.

"No humming," he said.

"I'm not." When he raised an eyebrow she bit her lower lip. "Sorry."

He did a mental count of his weapons. With limited

firepower and three people to cover, it was going to be tight. He knew who he wanted to sacrifice when the bullets started flying, but he'd somehow manage to save Trevor, too. Anything else would upset Sela, and Zach couldn't tolerate that.

Besides surviving the next few minutes, Zach had to get word to the team to take cover in case this was just a start to Vince's rampage.

Sela's focus hadn't strayed from Trevor. She ran a hand over his forehead and she tried to blot some of the blood from his face with the edge of her shirt. "Is he going to die?"

The "he" in question moved. A groan later Trevor lifted his hand and touched his forehead. "No."

Zach knew he should feel something for Trevor's seemingly miraculous recovery, but nothing came to him. "There, he said no. We can move on."

"I never thought I'd be happy to see you." Trevor blinked, his words slurring less the longer he talked.

"What happened?" Sela asked.

That was the last thing Zach wanted to talk about. "Never mind that. Who else is up there?"

With Sela's help, Trevor struggled to a sitting position. He leaned hard into her side. "Vince."

Zach ground his teeth together to keep from grabbing the guy and flinging him to the other side of the room. "Rod?"

"No." Trevor shook his head. A second later he put his hands over his ears and closed his eyes. "Nobody else that I could see. Just Vince."

Zach knew Trevor was trying to keep from passing

out or throwing up. Probably had a concussion, maybe something worse. "Trevor?"

"It's all been Vince." Trevor peeked at Sela. "All of it."

"What has?" she asked.

"Tell her, Trevor." Zach unstacked the two boxes beside him and moved stuff around inside, looking for anything that might help. "Let her see the real you."

"Zach, this isn't the time for a grudge." The fury in her voice matched the mass weighing him down.

He went right to the truth, didn't sugarcoat. "It could be the only time we have left."

She stood and walked to the bottom of the steps. Straining her neck, she looked up. "We should concentrate on getting out of here."

Zach wasn't ready to let Trevor's admission go. "How deep are you in this? Tell her."

When Zach just stood there and Sela joined him, Trevor shook his head. "Don't do this."

"Say it."

The silence drew out until Zach thought the other man would refuse to fill it. He was about to turn back to his fruitless box search when Trevor's gaze skipped over Sela and landed on the wall behind her.

"They had some information on me, about me. I had to get in the WitSec mess to keep it quiet."

"What is the information?" Zach barked out the question.

Something cold flashed in Trevor's eyes. "We need to get out of here."

"Is the door locked?" Sela asked.

Zach fought back the urge to shake the truth out of Trevor. "I'm guessing, but I'll check."

Trevor moved slowly and deliberately but at least he was in motion. "Any other exits?"

Zach had spent some time checking the place out when he'd started his work here. He had to know about the structure and feasibility of rocking the ground below a big house. The lack of a second exit always worried him. That meant one way out if he messed up. "Not from down here."

Sela sighed. "There has to be something here that can help us."

Zach was about to start up the stairs, facing bullets and whatever disaster loomed on the other side of the door, when he caught a flash out of the corner of his eye. Sela had taken over his job at the boxes. "Sela, don't."

"I am not going to sit here and die."

When faced with the impossible, she fought on. Zach respected her for that. If he were a different guy who hadn't seen what he'd seen, he might even love her. She was worth the battle and daily worry of losing her again.

And she deserved the truth, needed to hear it about Trevor so she'd understand that people really were black-and-white. Both sides warred in everyone, but a person had to choose. Trevor chose dark. Zach fought every day to keep out of the abyss, but it took all his strength and left nothing for anything else.

"Tell her, Trevor," Zach said.

Sela held up her hand. "I said stop."

If she had asked him in that pleading tone of hers, he would have caved, but her anger Zach could take. He continued to question Trevor. "What did they have on you? What made you sacrifice those women?"

Trevor sat on the floor, his legs unmoving, and shook his head. "I provided information only."

"And firepower."

Trevor exhaled, wincing as he did. "At times."

Zach refused to let it drop. Not now. Not when they were this close. "The blackmail was what?"

Sela turned away. She climbed into the pile, shoving boxes aside and digging in with such relish that the sound of ripping cardboard blocked out the conversation. "Zach, help me."

"With what?"

"There's a box back here." Her body went up and over the box she just tore apart. "About twenty of them actually." Her shoulders shook and the muscles in her neck strained as she tried to open something.

He gave in. "Let me help."

She stood over it, staring down as if a rabid scowl could open the box. "This one looks different. It's wood."

Zach didn't remember anything like that in the room. He'd glanced at the boxes when he stacked them out of the way at the start of the job. "Let me see."

"It's bolted shut." He tried to lift the lid but it didn't budge.

"Wait." She waved a finger in the air, then vaulted over the boxes and into the other room. "I saw a wrench."

"Convenient." The team accused him of finding conspiracies where they didn't exist, but having the only tool they needed be the one magically left behind struck him as part of a plan.

"What?" She shouted the question from the other room.

Zach nodded in Trevor's direction. "Any chance you can help here?"

"Get me up."

With an arm around Trevor's waist, Zach lifted from his knees, taking on the man's near-dead weight, but he didn't stop pushing his cause. "Tell her."

"Why does it matter now?" Trevor hissed out.

"She needs to know the truth about you."

"So then she'll hate me as much as you do?"

"Something like that."

She bounced back into the room, clearly fueled by a mix of adrenaline and fear. It made her slaphappy. "Here."

Trevor regained some strength with each step. By the time they got back to the wooden box, he'd shrugged out of his jacket and was pulling on the lid.

Zach didn't waste any time. His hands moved as fast as possible over the rusty bolts. With the final chinking sound as the metal hit the floor, both Zach and Trevor grabbed the edge and lifted.

Sela glanced over Zach's shoulder. "What is it?"

The smell hit him first. Rank and rotting, he recognized the stench of death. Through what looked like miles of plastic wrap and thick stretches of tape lay what once was a person. Releasing the lid brought the truth rushing to the surface.

Trevor's shoulders slumped. "Oh, damn."

When Zach felt Sela press herself up against him, his protective senses kicked into gear. "Step back."

Sela didn't move. Her face paled to the color of chalk. "Is that—"

"Yeah," Trevor said.

Zach tugged at the tape. Slipping the knife out of his back pocket, he clicked the blade open and sliced through the crinkling plastic.

"Who?" Sela covered her mouth with both hands but Zach could hear the question.

Answering her was what killed him. "Rod."

"Are you sure?"

Guilt and rage crashed through him. All those doubts about Rod's loyalty, all that anger about how he left them. And he'd been dead the whole time. Zach wanted to smash through the stone walls with his bare fists, punch them until they bled and he didn't feel anything.

He swallowed down the conflicting emotions flooding through him, forcing his mind and body to wipe clean. "I know the watch. I have one just like it. All the Recovery agents do."

It was all he could stand to look at. He didn't want to see Rod's face or what was left of him.

"It could be—"

Zach felt Sela's hand rubbing against his back and wondered how long she'd been touching him. "It's Rod."

Trevor backed up until he leaned against the wall. "I assumed, but seeing this…"

Zach shook his head, fought to keep out the darkness that threatened to swallow him. "It's too much. It never ends."

"Zach, it's okay," she said.

"It has to end now." Zach focused all of his energy on Trevor. "Tell her."

"It doesn't have anything to do with Rod."

"It has something to do with the situation we're in." Zach didn't know how, but it did.

Trevor didn't say anything for a few minutes. When he finally did, his voice was low and flat. "A tape."

Zach's mind sputtered. "What?"

"When my marriage broke apart we had an understanding. I wrote checks and she kept her mouth shut. Then one day she decided there was more money in talking than keeping quiet and used our son to get her way."

"What does this have to do with WitSec?" Sela asked.

Trevor shook his head, closing his eyes as his face grew darker. "In a drunken mistake, I talked with Russell Ambrose, a guy high up in witness protection."

Sela's eyes narrowed. "You don't drink."

"Not anymore."

The admission let Zach shift his focus. If he didn't know better, he would say that was Trevor's goal. To provide a focus on something other than death. "What was on the tape?

Trevor stared back with a bleak, desperate look in his eyes. In that moment he was a man who had lost everything. The money and power didn't matter. He spilled his guts and each word made him look physically smaller to Zach. It was as if the other man was folding in on himself. Crumpling.

"Trevor?"

"A conversation about making my wife disappear."

Sela's eyes closed as she let out a long breath. "Oh, Trevor."

Trevor switched to pleading. Still shaky on his feet, he used his hands and voice to get his point across. "My son means everything."

Zach wasn't in the mood for any of it. He snapped back to the present. They had bigger issues than Trevor's questionable morals.

Rod was dead. Just thinking the words pushed a crushing weight down on Zach's chest. He'd figure out how to deal with that pain later. Right now he needed to make sure Vince didn't add to his body count. He'd caused enough destruction.

And Zach would make sure he paid for it. "Save the speeches for another time. We need a plan."

"Cause a scene and lure Vince down here."

Trevor voiced the very plan Zach formed in his head.

Sela glanced back and forth between the men. "What if he's not here?"

"Then we could walk right out that door, which is why I'm betting he's here. He can't afford to let us escape." Zach tried to imagine what Vince was thinking and doing. "He has to make sure all the evidence is gone this time."

Sela rubbed her hands over her arms. "Evidence?"

"Witnesses," Trevor explained.

"A diversion," Zach said, ignoring the way fear tugged at the corners of her mouth. He had to stay focused. "We bring him down and we have a chance of taking him out."

Sela stepped in front of Zach, her eyes searching his face. "Or he could hurt you."

"Always a possibility."

"No." She shook her head hard. "Not one I'm willing to accept."

"I'll play dead." Trevor's voice boomed through the small space.

Zach didn't argue. It made sense. Trevor was debilitated from his fall. He wouldn't be able to stage a fight but he might be able to get off a shot or draw attention long enough for Zach to have a chance. "I need a gun." Trevor held out his hand. "Vince has mine."

"Not sure I trust you with one." Zach still wavered on Trevor. Sure, he was hurt, but the man played games. He could be involved with Vince even now and plotting his own takedown.

"I'm not going to let anything happen to Sela."

It was the one thing Trevor could say to change Zach's mind. He saw the way Trevor had shifted closer to her. The pose wasn't threatening. It was more paternal, like Trevor was doing what he could to shelter her.

But it wasn't enough. "Why?"

"Zach!" Red-cheeked and furious, Sela laid into him. "You can't still believe…"

Zach wanted to hear Trevor say it. Wanted Sela to hear the piece Zach knew in his heart to be true. That there was one part about Trevor she got right. "Why?"

"Because she supported me without question, never caring about the money, and offered her loyalty." The words rushed out of Trevor. "She was the only person who never wanted anything from me."

Satisfied, Zach nodded. "Then it's time to pay her back."

"We'll need a signal."

He had the perfect one. "Sela will do that."

"Me?"

"It's time that humming of yours comes in handy."

ADAM STOOD AT THE PASSENGER'S side of Luke's car outside Vince's house and rested his arms on top. "Vince slipped surveillance, not a trace of him in there or a clue as to where he went. Just a broken basement window from where he snuck out. And Zach's gone dark. Ever get the feeling you're in the middle of a setup?"

Luke couldn't shut off the ringing in his ears or the slow burn in his gut. "Almost every day."

"Where now?"

"You still can't get through to Zach?"

"Yeah, but that doesn't necessarily mean anything. He warned us he'd be underground, and that plays with the watch."

Luke wasn't buying the outward-calm act. He knew Adam harbored the same fears. "When was the last time the watches failed?"

"Never."

"Right. You made them. They are your baby. You took into consideration things like underground rooms. It's never been an issue before."

Adam nodded. "So, we go to Zach. To last place we knew his location."

They didn't have a choice. This was about tying up loose ends. That made them all a target but put Sela and Zach right in the line of fire. Taking them out could buy time for Vince to leave town. To get away.

Luke couldn't let that happen. "We go in with guns up, with one finger on the police emergency number."

"You're thinking this is going to go bad."

"It's the final play. If this is Vince, and I think we both know it is, he'll have the big guns out. He'll have planned this."

Adam swore. "He's going to take out Sela."

"And anyone with her, which means Zach."

"Let's go."

Chapter Sixteen

Sela screamed on queue.

Zach launched across the floor, nailing Trevor right in the stomach. The move sent them both flying back into the stack of cardboard boxes. Trevor groaned and the boxes crumpled over top of him.

His head shaking, Trevor dove for Zach's knees. They crashed against the boxes and into the wall. Through the thuds and yelling, the harsh name calling and pounding of fists, Sela watched the door. The goal was to make noise—a lot of noise—and bring Vince running.

The crashing, the thundering booms and bangs, it all ricocheted around her until she had to cover her ears with her hands. For a game, the rage between the men looked real. They weren't just making noise. They were working out whatever issues brewed between them.

But she knew Zach was holding back. He was stronger, younger and not hampered by a fall down the stairs like Trevor. Zach could have finished Trevor without much of an effort. That he kept from actually hurting Trevor was for her as much as for their plan.

Zach threw a box against the wall with a deafening crash. Slipping his gun out of his pocket, he fired a shot into the far corner. The echoing ricochet had them all ducking.

Then silence.

Trevor lay on his stomach, still, blood obvious on his shirt and hands, a gun a few feet from his waist.

For a second she thought Zach had slipped and actually killed Trevor. She started to go to him until she saw the sharp shake of Zach's head. His chest rose and fell on rough breaths and his left arm hung loose at his side. She didn't know if he was really hurt or just acting, but both men looked like they'd survived a fight to near death.

"I wondered who would come through that. For what it's worth, I'm happy it's you."

Vince was halfway down the stairs with a gun aimed at Sela's head before she even heard him.

Zach turned around slowly, his finger never leaving the trigger on his weapon. "Thought you'd be gone by now."

"Soon." Vince nodded at Zach's arm. "Drop the gun and kick it to me."

"Never."

"I'll put a bullet in your pretty girlfriend. You know my shot is as good as yours."

Zach just stood there. He didn't bring up his arm or follow the order. "Tell me something, Vince."

"Go ahead. You've earned the right to a few answers before you die."

"Was it all about the money?"

Vince smiled. If he was afraid or worried it didn't show. He stood long and lean like a man in charge, fearless in his decisions. "Selling information is a lucrative business."

"Pretty high price to pay for your soul."

"Spare me the crap. It was a business proposition, pure and simple. The secrecy of WitSec helped hide the bodies, and you would not believe what people will pay for that information." Vince smiled as he spoke.

Sela fought back the need to throw up. "You're sick."

"It's called ingenuity." He spied the gun on the floor. "Now, kick that to me. Zach, you're only wearing jeans but, knowing you, you're fully armed. I want all of the weapons or Sela gets a shot in the forehead."

Zach kept right on ignoring the older man. "Your actions killed people."

"Criminals."

"Innocent people."

Vince screwed up his mouth in a look of rabid distaste. "That's the Hollywood version of witness protection. The real-life version deals with criminals getting new lives and second chances on the taxpayer's dime."

Sela kept as still as possible. She focused on Zach's face instead of the gun pointed right at her. As Vince moved close, she wanted to bolt but she refused to show fear. They had a plan and it would work. It had to.

"We're supposed to believe this is about a cause?" Zach asked.

"Sure."

He shook his head. It was the only part of him that

had moved since Vince came down the stairs. "I don't buy it."

"I don't care."

"Ego."

Vince's eyes narrowed. "What?"

"This was about proving you could do it. About being smarter than everyone else."

Vince barked out a laugh. "And I was."

"You killed Rod." The words ripped out of Zach.

It was the one time she saw his control waver. Through clenched teeth, he referenced the man she now knew meant so much to him.

"Rod figured out someone was cashing in on WitSec information. He told me about the list of participants he had compiled and I knew he'd eventually trace it all back to me." Vince spoke with a cool detachment, like he was talking about a movie instead of a man whom he'd once called a friend.

The entire situation made Sela's stomach heave. Seeing Zach battle his inner demons, hearing Vince justify the unjustifiable.

"It was a great plan until Luke insisted on poking his nose in where it didn't belong." Just as Zach predicted, Vince talked. He reveled in what he viewed as his accomplishments.

"What now, Vince?"

"The house blows up. I'll be long gone before Rod is found."

"You've thought of everything." There wasn't any inflection in Zach's voice. He hid all emotion behind an unmoving body.

"It will just be part of a feud between two men over one very beautiful woman. People will know Zach had a job here and the equipment. The fact he's mentally on edge will explain the rest."

Sela's heart flipped over. "That's ridiculous."

Vince shrugged. "It just has to be believable enough to buy me time to get away. The plan is set. Vince will just disappear, never to be heard from again."

Through it all Zach remained stock-still. Not even a pinky twitched. "You're leaving the country."

"I spent a lot of time becoming an expert in hiding people right here. Now I can put that knowledge to work for me."

"Luke will never stop looking for you," she whispered. She'd known Luke for a few days only and she knew that much. He would go without sleep and everything else to avenge Zach and Rod.

"He will if he wants that young family of his safe." Vince rocked back on his heels, clearly pleased with the plan he'd designed and what he viewed as his insights into the Recovery team. "I tried to get Trevor there to back off, but he kept checking into things and meeting with Luke."

"You worried they'd start working together."

Until Zach said the words that piece didn't make sense. She couldn't figure out why Vince was picking the loose ends he did. After all, Luke was more of a foe than she could ever be. Now she got it. He worried his enemies would meet in a joint resistance, so he sought to cut them off.

"It seemed far-fetched at first, but then Luke has

always had a knack for doing the opposite thing and having it work."

Zach didn't even blink. "You know I'm not going down without a fight."

"Which is why Sela will come stand with me. Come here, dear." Vince waved at her with his gun.

That was the one rule Zach insisted on. She did not get close enough for Vince to touch her. "No way."

"I have to hand it to you, Zach. I never figured you'd finally find a woman by poaching on a man like Trevor. You should have seen him when she went missing." Vince used his hands to mimic an explosion as his eyes went wide with amusement. "Lost his mind."

"There seems to be quite a lot of that going on right now," she whispered under her breath.

Vince shook his head. "I assure you, I'm sane."

"Just greedy." Zach's harsh words brought the attention back to him.

Sela assumed that was the point. He wanted Vince's eyes only on him.

"Call it what you want, but I put in my years, served the government all while collecting low pay and listening to jokes about how public officials never worked."

"This is because someone didn't appreciate you enough?" Zach asked.

"No one did, but I think we've chatted enough. Luke can't be that far away, so it's time to wrap this up." Vince stepped closer. "Now, Ms. Andrews."

She didn't wait for another opportunity. Pressing air into her lungs she hummed a high off-key note. Vince winced at the sudden sound as all hell broke loose.

Trevor swept up off the floor, grabbing the gun by his side as Zach stepped in front of Sela, blocking her view and protecting her from harm at the same time. Sela dropped to the ground, curling into a tight ball as Zach ordered, but she could see the fight.

When Vince saw Trevor's weapon, he hesitated. It was the opening Zach needed. He flew at the older man, putting all of his weight behind it. They both dropped. Zach and Vince rolled across the floor. Punches landed on the older man's hand and torso, but he didn't drop the gun. A shot went wide, pinging off the ceiling. Wrestling Vince to his back, Zach grabbed the hand with the gun and tried to slam it against the concrete floor. Just as Zach reached the knife in his pocket, Vince bucked him off and both men hit the floor.

Trevor followed the whole scene. He swayed on his feet, shifting from side to side as he blinked. He aimed the gun several times but as one man flipped over the other and arms flew, Trevor didn't take a shot.

Sela doubted he would be able to stand much longer, not after all the knocks to his head. The lack of color on his face suggested he was about to drop.

But the fight wasn't dying down. Zach and Vince scrambled and guns skidded across the floor. She couldn't tell who was armed but she knew she had to do something.

Jumping to her feet, she rushed to Trevor's side and grabbed his gun. He tried to say something but no sound came out. She couldn't hear anything but the thundering of blood as it whooshed through her body.

One minute she was standing with the weapon

between her hands, the next Vince's leg shot out and tripped her, bringing her slamming to the floor on her shoulder.

Both Zach and Vince dove for the gun. Vince had the advantage, throwing out his long arm and twisting her fingers as he pulled. She screamed out in pain as Vince got it free. Looking down her body, she saw Vince's bloodied face and the barrel of a gun pointed at her. When she blinked again, a crushing weight fell across her stomach. Trevor's body lay over hers, his shoulders slamming back into her chest as his body took the force of the bullet meant for her.

"No!" She screamed the word over and over.

Zach rose up behind Vince, a gun in his hand and pure madness in his eyes. A second later Vince's mouth flattened and he flipped over, firing as he went. Zach's bullet caught Vince right in the forehead, sending him falling like dead weight over her ankles.

"Sela." Zach rushed to her, pulling her free from the pile on top of her.

She tried to help him, to say something, but her brain wouldn't work. A wash of blood stained everything around them. Instead of pain, she felt nothing. Empty. Stunned.

"Are you hurt?" His hands moved all over her.

She shook her head, but the words still wouldn't come.

Zach pulled her in his arms, cradling her frozen body against his warm one. Rocking her back and forth, he whispered to her. Nothing registered but the soothing purr of his voice. He brought her back to life.

As he kissed her forehead, she glanced over at Trevor. "He jumped in front of me."

Until then Zach hadn't focused on anyone but her. When she spoke, he glanced up. He shook his head as if trying to clear it, like he'd forgotten Trevor was even there. "Just a second."

Shuffling on his knees, Zach got to Trevor and turned him over. His eyes were open, his breath shallow.

"He's alive," Zach called out, bringing her to his side. "We need to get him help and fast."

Her eyes filled with tears when she saw the dark stain on Trevor's striped dress shirt. "Why'd you do it?" she asked him.

"Penance," he whispered.

"We'll get you out of here," Zach promised.

When he went to stand, Trevor grabbed his arm. Through harsh pants and a wheeze that rattled his bones, he spoke. "The explosives. Vince told me he was taking the house down."

"I haven't forgotten."

Sela had hoped that was all talk. "Are you sure that was real?"

When Zach lifted his head, a new determination filled his gaze. "Vince rigged the place to blow."

The roller coaster of emotions went racing through her again. One minute relief and the next terror. "We're not free yet."

"No."

She squeezed Trevor's hand, hoping he would hold on. "What are we going to do?"

Zach grabbed the other weapon off the floor and did a quick check for Vince's pulse. "This happens to be my area of expertise."

"And?" she asked.

Zach searched Vince's pockets. "Not sure yet."

She knew Zach did everything for a reason, but this wasn't making any sense to her. They didn't have time to check for evidence. Not now. "What are you doing?"

"Looking for a timer or something to set off the bomb. Something that will tell me what we're dealing with."

"Find anything?"

"No, but it can't be too intricate. This isn't Vince's area."

"I guess that's some good news."

Zach winked at her. "You keep thinking positive."

LUKE LOOKED OVER Adam's shoulder. They were stationed outside of the mansion, just out of sight from the front door in case someone came through with guns firing. "What do you see?"

Adam lowered the night-vision goggles. "No movement but we saw Trevor's car come in."

"That explains why he's not answering his phone. He's too busy causing trouble."

"Vince is in the wind. Trevor is where he's not supposed to be." Adam slipped on his Kevlar vest. "What's the plan here?"

"Heat scan?"

Adam glanced at his watch. "I can't get a read on

the basement. Something is blurring the information. Could be a few people in there."

"Then we go in large and loud."

"And if Vince has a small army in there?"

Luke knew they didn't have a choice. "We take them out."

"That's positive thinking."

"The alternative isn't worth discussing."

Chapter Seventeen

Zach brushed his hand over the door separating the basement from the floor upstairs. He didn't know where the explosives, bomb or whatever it was had been rigged or how, but he knew it was somewhere Vince could move around and get out fast. For his cover story to have any hope and for his desired effect of having the building come down, he had to have a lot of firepower well placed. That likely meant the top of the basement door.

He pushed the door and felt it hit against something. The edge of a can peeked through. He recognized it. His own equipment. Blasting agents, the ammonium nitrate fuel mixture. It was a bomb and that meant Vince needed a detonator. Also meant it was likely he planned to arm the bomb as he stepped out of the basement.

Footsteps sounded on the tile so soft that Zach would have missed them if he weren't plastered against the door. Zach could see shadows moving around. Two of them, moving in tandem without making a sound. He recognized the moves; the two were experts. That either meant that reinforcements had arrived or Vince brought in his own set of guns to make sure this operation went as planned.

Rather than shoot first and ask later, Zach tapped the button on his watch, hoping whatever blocked his communication earlier could get through now.

Nothing happened. He took the watch off and slipped the very edge under the door. Someone looking could miss it. No one on his team would. They'd recognize it for the message it was.

The figures stilled. "Zach?"

Relief rolled over Zach at the sound of Luke's voice. That fast, all the tension eased out of Zach's shoulders. He leaned his head against the door. "Yes."

"Khost." Luke whispered the code word and waited for Zach to say the safety word back.

Use the wrong one and they would think he was a hostage. The right one meant all clear. It was a backup system they rarely needed thanks to the watches. Zach had thought it useless but now he privately thanked Luke for his duplicate systems.

"Grenade."

"Good to hear your voice, man," Adam said.

Luke was all business. "We've got a mess out here."

Zach rushed to explain before anyone touched anything. "Vince set up a bomb. That was his plan to end this. Literally with a bang."

"Not all that original. Where is he?" Luke asked.

Zach looked down the dark staircase to Sela below. She had Trevor's head on her lap and was quietly talking to him. He thought she might even be singing.

"Dead at the bottom of the stairs."

"Good," Adam said. "Sela?"

"Fine, but Trevor is hurt."

"Again, good."

Usually Zach would agree. This time he didn't. For all the bad in the guy, at the end he did something good. "He saved Sela."

Luke cleared his throat. "Then let's get you out."

Exhaustion overtook Zach but he fought through it. Just a few more minutes and they'd all be free. "I'll walk you through this."

Chapter Eighteen

Trevor looked dead.

Sela stood at the end of his bed and stared at him as he lay still against the white hospital sheets. Machines tracked his vital signs and chimed with his steady heart-beat. He'd survived the surgery and would be fine. She wondered if she would be.

Zach appeared at her shoulder with his steady hand on her lower back. "Are you ready to go?"

She knew he hated it there, that he hated Trevor. But despite all the harsh words the men had exchanged, and the violence that had transpired, when everything fell apart Trevor stepped up and Zach returned the favor by getting him help. Luke pushed off questions from law enforcement, buying Trevor some time. Soon an invisible clock would chime and Trevor would have to face his future. The demons racing after him since his separation had pounced and caught him.

"What will happen to him now?" she asked Zach.

Trevor answered without opening his eyes. "He goes back to work."

He was still in denial and it made her sick. He'd done

awful things for reasons he'd convinced himself were right. He'd put her in danger. He'd almost robbed his son of his mother. He'd put all of the Recovery agents and their loved ones in the line of fire. He'd sent men to their slaughter, all in the name of keeping secrets.

The sins piled up until they smothered Sela. She had no idea how he could live with any of it, much less all of it. "You have to talk to the police," she pointed out.

Trevor hit the button on the remote next to his hand and his bed shifted. A whirring sound filled the room as his head lifted and his eyes opened. "We can handle that later."

"We?" Zach's voice was deadly hollow as he asked the question.

"Not you." Trevor's face paled when he nodded in her direction. "Sela."

No, not again. Never again. "I can't work for you. You know that, right?"

"The WitSec scam is over—"

"No." There was nothing confusing about Zach's response that time.

"Zach, stop." She pulled out of his hold and stood at the left side of Trevor's bed. "I appreciate everything you did for me, for the faith you showed in me, but it's not enough. When I weigh it against all the bad, it still comes up short. I can't keep working for you."

"We can put all of this behind us." His words came out firm, but the stormy sadness behind Trevor's eyes told a different story.

She took a deep breath and dove in. She'd never find the write words so she went with the honest ones.

"I'll never know if you're plotting or scheming. Never know if the files I'm compiling are for a new version of a WitSec scam. I can't live like that. Won't live like that."

"None of that is going to happen." He held the remote in a death grip. "A smart man learns his lesson and moves on."

"I hope so." Zach blew out a long breath as he shifted position to stand on the opposite side of Trevor's bed. "Because this is over."

Trevor tried to nod, but the brace around his neck stopped the movement. "I agree."

"He's talking about all of it." Luke stepped into the room and closed the door behind him. He held up a tape. "Every part of this ends now."

Trevor's eyes narrowed. "You have it."

"It was in a safe at Vince's house." Luke threw it and it landed with a soft thud on Trevor's chest. "Adam retrieved it."

Seeing Luke hand over the evidence sent a cold chill running through her. "Luke, what are you—"

He held up a hand. "It's a copy. Recovery will keep the original."

"Why?" Trevor asked, his voice sharp and his response swift.

"As insurance. Maybe as a reminder." Luke glanced at Zach and didn't continue until he nodded. "You're free, Trevor."

Trevor's eyes narrowed. "Meaning?"

"You go back to being an upstanding businessman who gives to charity, or as I like to call it, living the lie." A muscle in Zach's cheek twitched as he talked. "Just as you always hoped, you get away with it. You come out clean, your reputation intact."

Emotions warred inside of her. She cared about Trevor and still believed there was good in him. Throwing his body in front of hers, taking the bullet meant for her, proved that. But she now knew about the darkness. "What are you talking about?"

"No one will ever know about Trevor's role, except as our partner in jointly solving the WitSec murders and ferreting out the conspiracy," Zach said.

The anger and confusion fell away from Trevor's voice, leaving only a blank slate. "Why?"

"Because there's enough accountability. Because WitSec needs to be restored. Because the devastation needs to end." Luke rested his palms against the end of the bed and leaned in closer. "Because I had a talk with Congressman Brennan and he agreed the scandal would cause more damage, and WitSec is too tenuous to risk that right now."

Trevor's expression didn't change. "The congressman?"

"Yeah, your days of working for our government are over." Luke gave the other man a half smile of victory. "Good thing your company is diversified."

She couldn't process what they were saying. The words went in, relief swelled, but a part of her wondered if this was the right outcome. She saw Zach's drawn face and worried this would eat at him. Could a man who traveled in a black-and-white world tolerate this much gray? She doubted it.

"But mostly, Trevor, and I need you to understand this—" Zach stood there in silence for a few beats "—because you saved Sela."

"Zach, Luke." Her gaze traveled between them. "No." She couldn't live with that guilt. She didn't want that kind of burden on her shoulders.

Zach never broke eye contact with Trevor. "In his own deranged way he did assist Recovery. He gave us information even as he hid the pieces that would incriminate him."

"That all came after he tried to break into my house," Luke said.

Trevor sat up straighter. "Agreed."

"This isn't a new deal, Trevor. It's an end and an absolution for past sins, but anything from here and we hang you." Luke glanced at the tape. "And don't be dumb enough to think I only have one copy."

"Never forget people are watching," Zach said.

"Fair enough." Trevor turned to her. His hand inched toward where hers rested on the bed then pulled back. "Never forget that they did this for you. You might not think you're worth it, but they do. They know."

Her eyes filled with tears. She'd suppressed all the pain and confusion for the last few days. Now it flowed through her and stopping it took all her energy. "Trevor—"

"One day you'll understand." He patted the mattress before clearing his voice. "Luke, we likely have a story to create."

"Yeah."

Sela wanted to stay, wanted to dissect everything

that had happened and make it fit in her head. Then she looked at Zach, saw his broad shoulders and the softness hidden in his hard face, and her priorities shifted. Trevor was her past, all jumbled and twisted. Zach was her future, or she wanted him to be, dared to hope he would be. Convincing him was the key.

"Let's step outside." Zach motioned for Sela to follow him out of the room.

She glanced at Trevor one last time and in her heart and mind let go. "Goodbye, Trevor."

He smiled. "Good luck, Sela."

ZACH WANTED TO WRAP Sela up, bundle her against the disappointment, and run to anywhere that wasn't here. She needed a guy who was good at this stuff, who understood emotions and could make it all better. He wasn't that guy.

He walked her toward the elevator with his hands against her elbow. Silence spun around them even as the hospital floor buzzed with activity and constant noise. He heard only the thumping of his heart and the shallow breathing in his chest.

He hit the down button and stared at the closed doors in front of him. Searching for the right words to say, for the right way to comfort her, burned in his gut like acid.

She broke the informal no-talking pact. "Now what?"

"Luke and Trevor will—"

She threw an arm in front of Zach when the doors

opened and nodded for the man inside to go on without them. "Not that."

"What?"

"Are you kidding?"

He watched the doors close again. "I don't understand the problem."

She breathed in deep enough for him to see her chest expand. "Us, Zach."

This was the wrong place and definitely the wrong time. "Let's get home."

"And where is that exactly?"

"I still don't—"

"Do I come home with you, go back to my apartment, go to the warehouse…give me a clue here, Zach. Where do you see me?"

"You can come home with me, if you want." When her cheeks flamed red he knew he'd given the wrong answer.

"What do you want?"

When a worker pushing a food cart nearly ran them over, Zach maneuvered them out of the hallway and into the small lounge at the end of the hall. No one sat in the dank space, but the television blared. He turned it off then faced Sela again. "Tell me what you want me to say."

She shook her head. "It doesn't work that way."

"It does for me."

"Because you never see gray."

He had no idea how the conversation had veered into this territory. "I'm sorry?"

She stepped up until she stood right in front of him,

her shoes touching his. "I want you to take a chance on me."

The words cut right through him to the icy place he denied and ran from at every opportunity. "We'll date."

"Really?"

It sounded right to him. Normal. "Isn't that what people do?"

"What scares me is that you don't even know the answer to that."

"Maybe we should take a deep breath, get something to eat—"

"Food isn't going to fix this."

"I still don't know what 'this' is." If he denied it, weaved and ducked, he could get them back on track. They could see each other and he could play the game that everyone else was living.

"How do you feel about me?"

Like he would shatter if he didn't see her. Like he would shatter if he did. "I like you."

She barked out a laugh. "That's it?"

"It's a lot." He shook his head, battling the voices inside him. He could tell her just a bit, let her see the anger, then she would get it. "When I was in Afghanistan there was this explosion. Not unusual since things blew up all the time. I turned around and saw all these rocks piled at the entrance of this cave. Then I did this head count."

As he talked, his heart doubled its beat. The smell of death and gunfire. The shocking splash of red against the barren landscape that at first looked like paint until his vision cleared and he recognized it as blood. "I couldn't find Holden. Couldn't find a lot of the guys."

Her hand rested against Zach's chest. "They were trapped inside," she whispered.

"I dug with my gun, my hands, pulled and climbed until my skin was raw and my throat dry enough to crack. It took us days. We worked in groups, some of us keeping watch while others worked." He remembered the awful silence followed by the horrible screams. His friends were dying, running out of air and bleeding out, and he couldn't get there. "When I finally saw Holden…I'd never seen him like that, hovering on the brink of death and not knowing which side would be better. I got furious. I've been furious ever since."

Zach stepped away from her, from her soothing touch and sad eyes. "In war you learn to separate your brain from your feelings. You see death and know it's always out there, waiting. You live life knowing the worst is hovering and being prepared for it."

She rushed to him again. "I'm alive. I want to be alive with you."

"And I want to give you all I can." He meant that. With all he had and all he knew, he meant it.

Her hands dropped to her side as the light in her eyes died. "But you can't let me in."

Women said stuff like that and his brain shut down. His ex-wife had once whispered a similar phrase. Then he didn't care. He got angry, built a wall and shut her out. He wanted to do that with Sela but with every brick he set in place another one crumbled. "You're as far in as anyone is going to get."

"No."

"No?"

"Last year that might have been okay. Might have been enough. My life was upside down and my self-worth in the toilet, but that's over. I'm not living from minute to minute anymore. I want a future. A real one."

He had no idea what to say or how to keep her tethered to him. She wanted some huge declaration and had no idea what she was asking for. If she saw the real him, the rage he tucked down deep, she'd run away and he wouldn't blame her. "I don't disagree."

"I deserve more." She turned toward the door.

Knowing she would one day leave and watching her do it were two different things. His heart lodged in his throat as anxiety bubbled up in his stomach. "I'm not the one who's running here."

"That just shows you're not getting it."

"Because?"

"You deserve more, too. Whatever man you were, you've put the pieces back together again, and you deserve a future, not just a past."

"I'm fine with my life."

The last flicker of light left her face. "That's what's killing me."

Chapter Nineteen

Sela slipped away from the party and headed upstairs to the warehouse loft. In the open layout, the music rose as did the din of laughter and conversation.

After the hysteria had died down, the team decompressed. Mia had announced it was time to get married. A week after they buried Rod, they celebrated Mia and Holden's marriage. The more public celebration gave way to a private one, team members only, at the warehouse.

After that, Mia and Holden would sneak away for a week. The rest of them would finish setting up their secure houses and try to start normal lives while they worked every minute with danger.

Luke would do what he did best. Manage them all. With their reputations intact from uncovering the WitSec fiasco and Rod's name clear, Luke would line up new work.

He had to testify before a specially convened security panel in Congress about the WitSec affair. As promised, he would keep Trevor's name out of it. If her former boss wanted to come clean, that would be his choice. By saving her, he'd bought his freedom from the wrath of the Recovery Project.

The finality continued with her. This would be her last night in the warehouse or anywhere with Zach. After the informal wedding reception, she'd sneak out. Return to her apartment and try to put her life back together. For a brief flash she'd let herself believe she'd found something with Zach, but no matter how much she pounded he would not open the door and let her in. His idea of her as some sort of fun-time office girl had changed almost immediately, but his priorities hadn't. He rescued and retreated.

She'd seen him do it over the past two weeks. He'd make love to her with abandon, then distance himself during the day.

"Are you okay?" he asked as he slipped behind her and wrapped his arms around her waist.

She was brokenhearted and sad. With her insides ripped and bleeding, she gave him the truth. "Just packing."

"Why?

Typical Zach. No arguments or pleading. They'd talked about this at the hospital and he pretended it never happened. He lived the days as if they were going forward on his terms. "It's time for me to go back to my life."

"You're unemployed."

That was the least of her concerns. She had no idea where to go from here. Trevor insisted she still had a job, but she couldn't go back to Orion now. Not with what she knew. Understanding the choices he'd made didn't come easy. Accepting them or pretending they hadn't happened was impossible.

Trevor had put her in danger, stolen her sense of security, but he had also restored her faith that people could be good when he threw himself in front of her. The press cheered him for it. She gave him her gratitude right before saying goodbye. He would live but she wanted no part of that future.

"Luke said he would help me get started again. He has some contacts and will give me a reference, even though he'll have to fake his way through it since I never worked for him." She appreciated the offer. One day when the bills piled up and her heart healed, she would venture out and find something.

Zach turned her around in his arms. "You didn't have to go to Luke. I would have helped."

Because that's what he did. It was who Zach was. He fixed. "Luke volunteered."

"You can be an assistant here." Zach blurted out the sentence. It was as if he said it right as he thought it.

The idea was so tempting. Seeing him every day would be both sweet and torturous. "No."

His arms closed tighter around her. "We need someone to keep everything in order and—"

"Stop." She put her hand over his mouth when he went to kiss her. One touch of his lips and she'd lose her nerve. She needed it now.

He pulled his head back. "What?"

"Is that where you think we are? That I want a job from you?"

"I—I'm trying to help." He stuttered, actually

tripped over his words for the first time since she'd met him.

"I know."

"What, you'll accept help from Luke but not from me?"

She didn't love Luke. She loved Zach and that made all the difference. Gone were the moments where she would go along to see where he would take her.

In the short time she'd known him she'd come to see him as this multifaceted, complex man worth loving. His strength and decency had won her over.

But he only saw himself one way. "You're rescuing again."

He smiled. "Is that so bad?"

"It is if you use it as a wall."

His mouth turned down and his arms loosened around her waist. "I don't know what you're talking about."

She wondered if that was true, if he buried it all so deep that he didn't even recognize the defense mechanism anymore. Maybe it was natural to him. Maybe it felt right. Still, she'd stood at that wedding and watched them all celebrate while Zach held back, a small smile on his face.

He loved them, but he had no idea what to say to them. That much was clear.

The opposite wasn't true. They'd brought him into their circle. Claire and Mia had cajoled and pestered until Zach had finally hit the dance floor. Maddie had joked with him like an annoying little sister who really adored her older brother. Avery had respected his need for space and sent him a wink instead of crushing him in hugs.

The women, the men, they all let him have the air he needed. Instead of using that time to accept, he hid behind it.

She didn't want that detachment.

"Let me understand this." She reached behind her and broke his hold. Stepping out of the comforting circle of his arms, she could face what she had to say. Make her point and see if he snapped to life. "We're going to work together. You'll come in and I'll get you coffee, hand you files. Is that your plan?"

"Yeah."

The word sliced through her. "I take notes and we joke around, just like I do with Adam, and he barely likes me."

"He likes you fine."

"That's not my point and you know it."

"It's more than that."

She wanted so badly for that to be true. "Tell me. Explain it to me."

"Why are we talking about this?"

He could fight with weapons but words seemed to fail him when she challenged him. "It's your plan, Zach. Tell me how it will work."

"I don't know."

"Sex."

His eyes widened. "Could you not yell that?"

"That's the plan, right? We have some dinners, continue to have sex."

"Isn't that what dating is?"

"What happens when I start dating other men?"

His face fell. Eyes, cheeks, mouth all into a flat line. "What?"

In her heart she wanted to give him time and to accept whatever he could offer, but in her head she knew he would wade in the status quo unless shoved. So she pushed. "I'm twenty-five. I want a life. Stability, kids."

The area around his mouth went white. "Okay."

"That's all you have to say?" She could see him swallow.

"There's nothing stable about my life."

She threw her arms wide. "Look around you. Luke is going to be a father. Holden and Caleb are husbands. Adam is steps away from getting there. You're the only one holding back despite the dangers."

"I'm not them."

"No, you're right. They're not afraid." She could no longer hear the music or the talking from downstairs. It was just the two of them, locked in a battle for the future.

"Are you trying to piss me off?"

Any emotion was a win at this point. "I'm trying to wake you up."

"We can date. I've thought about it and that makes the most sense. We date."

The words knocked against her heart, hard, as if he'd hit her with a stick. Silence beat around them. She knew then the crowd downstairs was listening in. The music hummed low in the background, but quiet filled the space as if they were all holding their collective breath. "And then what?"

"I don't know."

"Because you still don't see a future. You don't let yourself dream and believe. Your heart is locked back in that cave in Afghanistan."

She knew about those dark days. The night after they'd buried Rod, Zach had talked even more about knowing Holden was on the other side of that mountain tunnel but not knowing if he was alive or dead.

The story gave her hope. It had given her a brief glimpse into the depth of his feeling. She knew he could grieve and feel; he just fought it with everything he had. "You open your soul to your friends here, but only so much."

"I don't know what you want from me."

"And that's the problem."

"You want a mind reader, Sela. Tell me and I'll try to give it to you."

"What?"

"Whatever it is you need."

He thought it was that simple. She would hand him a checklist and he would try to match it. "I want a man who will leap with me. Maybe not today or this year, but I have to know it can happen. That he wants to try."

He swore under his breath. "And people say I'm cryptic."

"I used to think so. I don't anymore."

"What does that mean?"

"You're scared."

He dropped onto the bed with his elbows on his

knees and his hands hanging down. "Insults aren't going to fix this."

"No, nothing is." She leaned over, her heart full and her eyes burning, and kissed him on the top of the head. "Good night, Zach."

"You mean goodbye."

She reached the top of the steps and turned around. "Yeah."

LUKE STEPPED UP BESIDE ZACH when he came downstairs and handed him a beer. "You know this is a party, right?"

Zach couldn't take his eyes off Sela. She'd made some stupid ultimatum, one he didn't even know was a big deal until she walked out. Seeing her go down those stairs took something from him. He'd gone from feeling lighter, calmer, to fighting the old battle with anxiety.

"Sure." He didn't even know what question he was answering as he sipped on the drink.

"You're more quiet than usual."

"Is that a problem?"

Adam appeared on Zach's other side. "And strangely sensitive."

Zach reached down deep for control. He could not lose it now. Not here. Not in front of the only people in the world who mattered to him. "Sorry."

Adam shrugged. "I'll live."

"Sela." The syllables ripped out of Zach. It actually hurt to say her name.

Luke and Adam stared at each other, but only Luke spoke. "Excuse me?"

"She's leaving after the party." He couldn't believe after the past few days she'd go. He tried everything he could think of to bind her to him. They were together. He'd made love to her.

None of it was enough to hold her. She wanted what Luke had. What the rest of them had. She didn't understand that he wasn't them. That he had this anger he had to control.

"You're letting her go?" Adam asked.

"She's a grown woman."

"No question about that."

Zach knew without looking that Adam was watching Sela as he said it. "Don't."

"I'm not blind, but my real question was about why you aren't fighting to make her stay."

"She's not Claire. Not Maddie or any of them."

Luke's eyes narrowed. "True."

"She's young."

"Last I checked she was of age," Adam pointed out.

They weren't getting it. It wasn't really about her. It was about him. "I'm not that guy."

"I have no idea what that means." Adam leaned around Zach to look at Luke. "You?"

"None."

He kept trying to explain but no one was getting it. Sela acted like it didn't matter, like she actually was willing to see if he could go the distance.

For the first time he did wonder about her taste in men. Picking him had not been a great move. They were thrown together and, adrenaline or not, she should have open eyes by now.

"The couple thing?" He shook his head. "Not me."

"And you know this how?" Luke asked.

"What?"

"You have a lot of experience as a couple and I missed it?" Luke lowered his voice. "And don't tell me about your previous marriage. You were a kid and never around. That was playing house. I'm talking about a real relationship."

This wasn't about that. Zach knew that much. He could separate the bad choices of the past from what he felt for Sela. This was about a bigger issue with who he was and what he'd become.

He didn't just hunt bad guys, he enjoyed seeing them pay. It was bloodthirsty and totally beneath Sela. "She wants a husband and a normal life."

Adam seemed surprised at that one. "She wants to get married now?"

"Someday."

"To you?"

"I don't know."

Luke exhaled as he put his empty glass on the table next to him. "Seems to me you're skipping a few steps. Like the ones where you get to know each other."

Sela laughed and Zach could hear it across the room. The sound rushed through him, extinguishing some of the darkness. She nearly doubled over with her hand over her mouth. He didn't know what was so funny, but he wanted her to do it again.

He shook his head. This was nuts. He had to get out. "I'm getting a headache."

When he turned to leave, Luke grabbed his arm. "You deserve her, you know."

"I don't."

"You're one of the most decent men I know and you don't even realize it." Adam nodded in agreement to Luke's words.

Something clogged Zach's throat. "You don't—"

"Know you wrestle with anger? Know you think you've lost it and are unworthy and right on the edge? I get that. We all feel that way. It's the burn-off from what we do and the ghost from everything that came before. It doesn't mean you don't deserve her." Luke stared Zach down.

Adam grew serious. "Luke's right, man."

Zach looked back and forth between the men he viewed as brothers. They believed in him when he refused to believe in himself. He wanted to see what they saw, but he'd buried it for so long, afraid to lose one more thing, to fail to stop the deaths of the innocent and the people he cared about.

"Do you love her?" Luke's voice was calmer now, less confrontational.

"No." The word shot out of Zach's mouth automatically. He didn't think about the answer. He forced out the response before he could turn it over and tell the truth.

"Huh." Luke looked at Adam. "Then that settles it."

Adam nodded. "Maybe you're right. You aren't that guy."

Suddenly the idea of being ruled out for Sela didn't sit so well with Zach. "I could be."

If he wished it so, maybe he could make it so. If good men like Adam and Luke believed in him, if Sela was willing to fight for him, maybe he had a chance, after all.

"You just said you weren't," Luke said.

"I was making conversation." Zach stole another look at her. Dressed in a navy dress that hit right above her knees, she looked all clean and beautiful. He let his mind toy with the question. "I mean, a guy needs time. Right?"

"Yeah." Adam coughed over his answer.

Zach ignored his friends' obvious amusement. Let Luke and Adam think what they wanted. He kept his focus on Sela. "It hasn't been that long. We're talking weeks."

Luke suffered from the same coughing fit as Adam. "Right. Weeks."

"We should take our time. Not rush to go our separate ways." The more he talked, the more Zach liked the plan. She wanted all the answers today. He couldn't do that. He also couldn't think about her with another man without wanting to throw up.

Adam grabbed his drink and hid his mouth behind it. "Makes sense."

"It does." Zach slapped Luke on the shoulder. "So, Recovery."

Luke's smile faded. "You lost me right there."

"We're going to hire her."

"We are?" Luke took extra syllables to ask the question.

"That way she'll be here every day."

Adam elbowed Luke. "And not out dating other men."

"She'll be with me," Zach said.

"Have you told her this yet?" Luke asked.

"I suggested it but thought I should get your okay."

"Are you asking or telling me?"

Zach felt the anxiety racing around inside his brain cool down. "She can start in a week. She needs some time with me first."

Adam laughed. "Make sure you tell her that when you tell her about the job. She might say no."

"Will do." Zach was barely listening to his friends. Now that he had a plan, he wanted to put it into action.

Luke stopped him before he could go more than a few steps. "Zach?"

"What?"

"I hate to tell you this, but you already love her."

Zach waited for the panic to come. He usually heard the word and wanted to run. This time it felt right. "I know."

Chapter Twenty

Luke wrapped an arm around his wife and whispered into her ear. "We're going to want to watch this."

Claire rubbed her growing belly as she sipped on water. She stood a few feet away from Sela, listening to her talk about going over the balcony of the safe house in Zach's arms.

"What's going on?" Claire asked.

"Zach is about to tell Sela what she's doing for the rest of her life."

"The poor deluded man." But Claire smiled as she said it.

"That's the fun part."

She shrugged. "How do you figure that?"

Luke wrapped an arm around her. "She loves him."

"Maybe not after this."

He squeezed her shoulder. "Have faith."

"In you?" She kissed him. "Always."

"WHAT'S HAPPENING?" Sela walked over and kissed Luke on the cheek. It was a habit, one borne out of respect and gratitude. He held everything together while the world blew apart. She knew that was a special skill.

Luke nodded at something over her shoulder. "Zach is behind you."

She tried not to tense up. She'd been smiling so hard for the past hour, pretending everything was fine while breaking inside, that her cheeks ached. She didn't have much fake happiness left inside her. At this point she was held together with a bit of pluck and the tie to her wrap dress. Nothing more.

She turned around and sent a forced smile in Zach's direction. "Hi."

At the sound of her chirpy greeting everyone turned around. She wanted to go out with dignity, but that wasn't going to be possible now. Zach was going to push it. She could see it in the way he braced his legs apart and kept his hands on his hips.

"You're not leaving."

Someone groaned. Sela thought she heard Maddie whisper Zach's name. Sela thought both reactions were appropriate. "Excuse me?"

"I am not letting you go."

She was about to yell at him but bit back the response. His voice was firm, but those blue eyes carried a note of…fear. "Why?"

"I don't want you to go."

"Because I'm such a good secretary?"

"I don't even know if you can type."

"Oh, that's just great," Luke mumbled from behind her.

Sela blocked it all. She didn't care who watched,

but this showdown was between her and Zach. No one else. "I'm still not hearing anything more than I heard upstairs. You want to date. You want sex."

He winced at that one. "All true. I do, but I want more than that."

Hope flickered to life inside her chest. "Like?"

"I'm taking you up on your offer."

She had no idea what he was saying. "How romantic for me."

He took both her hands in hers. Until he touched her, she thought she could handle this. She could act like it didn't matter and hold her head up so as not to ruin the day for Mia and Holden. But being this close to Zach, smelling the soap on his skin and feeling the warm brush of his skin against hers, did her in.

"No more pretense, Zach. Just tell me."

"I want the chance. I'm not sure how good I'll be at this couple thing." He rested his forehead against hers. "Honestly, I have my doubts. About me, not you."

"I believe in you."

He placed a soft kiss on her lips. And when he pulled back, he looked at her with a smile that promised the world. "Take a chance on me."

She knew then. He loved her. He was jumping off that cliff with her because he did believe. He wouldn't ask, stand there in front of everyone and risk being turned down, unless he wanted it as much as she did. And it changed everything. Took all the pain and washed it away in a wave of hope.

She sniffed to keep the tears from flowing. "We need to be clear about one thing."

He frowned but wisely stayed quiet.

"I am taking the job here because it's right for me." She glanced over her shoulder at Luke. "And I can type."

He winked at her.

She went back to Zach. "Not because you are arranging my life. This is my choice."

"Got it."

"I don't need to be rescued."

"Sometimes you do."

"And so do you, but this is not about that."

"Okay."

"Besides, you need a keeper." She wrapped her arms around his neck. "I figure I'll have my hands full watching over you."

"I'm not sure Luke will pay you for that."

"Yes, I will." The whole room laughed at Luke's comment.

Sela felt it all—the love and acceptance. Every person in this room would die for the others. They'd banded together in a makeshift family that transcended blood ties.

She loved them but mostly she loved Zach. He filled her with sunshine and made all things seem possible. With him, she could face the past and embrace the future.

But it was time to torture him. "Now tell me."

"What?" He pretended to look terrified but couldn't hide his smile as he did it.

"Right here, in front of everyone. I want to hear it."

That made the amusement disappear. "Uh, Sela."

"It's time, Zach."

"Listen to the lady." Adam added a whistle to his comment.

"Fine." A smile lit up Zach's face. "I don't know how it happened so fast or even what it was until it knocked me on my butt, but I love you."

He said it with such ease, so fast, that the words almost didn't register. "Say it again."

He rolled his eyes. "Oh, come on."

"Please."

He picked her up off the floor until her eyes were even with his. "Listen up, Sela Andrews. I love you."

Within seconds they were swamped with hugs and good wishes. The men kissed her and the women talked about Zach taking the big fall. Sela soaked it all in. When Zach broke free from the group to spin her around, she laughed until she cried.

"I love you." She repeated the words as he kissed her.

When they came up for air, she knew everything would be okay. "I can hardly wait to get started on that future."

And she knew he meant it. "Let's sneak out of here and get started."

"It's not our wedding." He looked around. "But someday."

THREE DAYS LATER, Adam, Luke and Zach sat around the conference table. The women were off looking at the new apartment Adam was working on for him and Maddie.

"It's over. Congressman Brennan is happy. Maddie is safe and the idiot who paid to have her killed is facing a new load of charges. It looks as if we've found everyone involved in the scam and the cleanup of the program has begun." Luke gave the laundry list as he closed the thick folder in front of him.

"And Trevor Walters is getting a hero's welcome." Adam snarled as he said it.

Zach shrugged. "He is one."

"Excuse me?"

"He saved Sela." Zach knew that didn't wipe the slate clean. Trevor had done so many bad things, including threatening to kill his ex, but he stood up when it mattered. Zach wouldn't forget that. "Yeah, I know he caused—"

Adam held up his hand. "That's a good enough reason for me."

Luke nodded. "Me, too."

"So now we get back to business." Adam reached for the coffeepot behind him and started pouring a round for all of them.

"Which is?" Zach asked.

"These." Spinning around, Luke reached for a new stack of files next to the monitors. He dropped them on the table with a thud. "Brennan made some calls about cold cases and recent missing persons investigations. Looks like he found some work for us."

Adam fingered the folders. "And two private clients have contacted us, one a corporation missing a member of its management team and one a family."

The world had tilted right again. All those years of

running on the fringe came back to Zach. He wouldn't change much. He'd needed that time to heal and learn to battle the anger inside. With Sela's help and Mia dusting off her unused therapy skills for him, he'd get through. He'd learn to wrestle the rest of the beast down.

Until then he had everything else. A future. A love. A chance.

He swallowed the lump in his throat. This time he knew what it was. Satisfaction. Pure emotion.

He grabbed the top folder. "Looks like we've got plenty to keep us busy."

Luke looked at the pot and his cup. "We're going to need more coffee."

Zach smiled. Yeah, life was good.

* * * * *

Harlequin®

INTRIGUE®

COMING NEXT MONTH

Available October 11, 2011

#1305 MAJOR NANNY
Daddy Corps
Paula Graves

#1306 ENGAGED WITH THE BOSS
Situation: Christmas
Elle James

#1307 CLASSIFIED
Colby Agency: Secrets
Debra Webb

#1308 STRANGER, SEDUCER, PROTECTOR
Shivers: Vieux Carré Captives
Joanna Wayne

#1309 WESTIN LEGACY
Open Sky Ranch
Alice Sharpe

#1310 BLACK OPS BODYGUARD
Donna Young

HICNM0911

REQUEST YOUR FREE BOOKS!
2 FREE NOVELS PLUS 2 FREE GIFTS!

Harlequin®

INTRIGUE®

BREATHTAKING ROMANTIC SUSPENSE

YES! Please send me 2 FREE Harlequin Intrigue® novels and my 2 FREE gifts (gifts are worth about $10). After receiving them, if I don't wish to receive any more books, I can return the shipping statement marked "cancel." If I don't cancel, I will receive 6 brand-new novels every month and be billed just $4.49 per book in the U.S. or $5.24 per book in Canada. That's a saving of at least 14% off the cover price! It's quite a bargain! Shipping and handling is just 50¢ per book in the U.S. and 75¢ per book in Canada.* I understand that accepting the 2 free books and gifts places me under no obligation to buy anything. I can always return a shipment and cancel at any time. Even if I never buy another book, the two free books and gifts are mine to keep forever.

182/382 HDN FEQ2

Name	(PLEASE PRINT)
Address	Apt. #
City	State/Prov.	Zip/Postal Code

Signature (if under 18, a parent or guardian must sign)

Mail to the Reader Service:
IN U.S.A.: P.O. Box 1867, Buffalo, NY 14240-1867
IN CANADA: P.O. Box 609, Fort Erie, Ontario L2A 5X3

Not valid for current subscribers to Harlequin Intrigue books.

**Are you a subscriber to Harlequin Intrigue books
and want to receive the larger-print edition?
Call 1-800-873-8635 or visit www.ReaderService.com.**

* Terms and prices subject to change without notice. Prices do not include applicable taxes. Sales tax applicable in N.Y. Canadian residents will be charged applicable taxes. Offer not valid in Quebec. This offer is limited to one order per household. All orders subject to credit approval. Credit or debit balances in a customer's account(s) may be offset by any other outstanding balance owed by or to the customer. Please allow 4 to 6 weeks for delivery. Offer available while quantities last.

Your Privacy—The Reader Service is committed to protecting your privacy. Our Privacy Policy is available online at www.ReaderService.com or upon request from the Reader Service.

We make a portion of our mailing list available to reputable third parties that offer products we believe may interest you. If you prefer that we not exchange your name with third parties, or if you wish to clarify or modify your communication preferences, please visit us at www.ReaderService.com/consumerschoice or write to us at Reader Service Preference Service, P.O. Box 9062, Buffalo, NY 14269. Include your complete name and address.

HI11B

*Harlequin Romantic Suspense presents the latest book
in the scorching new* KELLEY LEGACY *miniseries
from best-loved veteran series author Carla Cassidy*

*Scandal is the name of the game as the Kelley family fights
to preserve their legacy, their hearts...and their lives.*

Read on for an excerpt from the fourth title
RANCHER UNDER COVER

*Available October 2011
from Harlequin Romantic Suspense*

"**W**ould you like a drink?" Caitlin asked as she walked to the minibar in the corner of the room. She felt as if she needed to chug a beer or two for courage.

"No, thanks. I'm not much of a drinking man," he replied.

She raised an eyebrow and looked at him curiously as she poured herself a glass of wine. "A ranch hand who doesn't enjoy a drink? I think maybe that's a first."

He smiled easily. "There was a six-month period in my life when I drank too much. I pulled myself out of the bottom of a bottle a little over seven years ago and I've never looked back."

"That's admirable, to know you have a problem and then fix it."

Those broad shoulders of his moved up and down in an easy shrug. "I don't know how admirable it was, all I knew at the time was that I had a choice to make between living and dying and I decided living was definitely more appealing."

She wanted to ask him what had happened preceding that six-month period that had plunged him into the bottom of the bottle, but she didn't want to know too much about him. Personal information might produce a false sense of intimacy that she didn't need, didn't want in her life.

"Please, sit down," she said, and gestured him to the table. She had never felt so on edge, so awkward in her life.

"After you," he replied.

She was aware of his gaze intensely focused on her as she rounded the table and sat in the chair, and she wanted to tell him to stop looking at her as if she were a delectable dessert he intended to savor later.

Watch Caitlin and Rhett's sensual saga unfold amidst the shocking, ripped-from-the-headlines drama of the Kelley Legacy miniseries in

RANCHER UNDER COVER

*Available October 2011
only from Harlequin Romantic Suspense,
wherever books are sold.*

SPECIAL EDITION

Life, Love and Family

Look for
NEW YORK TIMES AND *USA TODAY*
BESTSELLING AUTHOR

KATHLEEN EAGLE

in October!

Recently released and wounded war vet
Cal Cougar is determined to start his recovery—
inside and out. There's no better place than the
Double D Ranch to begin the journey.
Cal discovers firsthand how extraordinary the
ranch really is when he meets a struggling single
mom and her very special child.

ONE BRAVE COWBOY,
available September 27 wherever books are sold!